Typesetting by Janice Lee
Cover Photo by Jay Halsey
Cover Design by Michael Seidlinger
Special Thanks to Irene Doukas Behrman
Copyediting by Esa Grigsby
ISBN 978-1-948700-19-1

THE ACCOMPLICES:
A Civil Coping Mechanisms Book
🐱 🐱 🐱

theaccomplices.org

THE ACCOMPLICES

Ghosts Are Just Strangers Who Know How to Knock

by Hillary Leftwich

For Cobain
To the moon and the stars and back again

TABLE OF CONTENTS

Somewhere There Is a Field Where the Birds Will Die for You **11**

A Small Infestation Following a Big Stroke of Luck   **12**

Praise the Lord and Pass the Ammunition   **15**

I Lost My Orgasm   **17**

Things They Don't Talk About in Parenting Class   **18**

Runt   **19**

Huckleberry   **20**

dead boys   **21**

Loss Aversion   **23**

The Dead Room   **24**

Bottle Rockets   **25**

The Difference Between a Raven and a Crow   **28**

Lullaby   **29**

Holes   **31**

His Bones   **32**

Supertramp   **34**

Saba on the Shore   **35**

The Ocean Resonates in Empty Spaces   **37**

Paladin   **38**

You Can Always Come Back   **40**

Wild Hares   **45**

Bang, Snap!   **46**

Final Trumpet   **49**

Lifespan **50**

I answer the missed connections on Craigslist because I don't want people to feel alone and I don't want to feel alone either **51**

Examination **52**

Rockabye Sweet Baby James **56**

Northern Lights **57**

People Call You a Space Cowboy **60**

Ghosts **61**

Tajo **62**

If Only Tonight We Could Sleep **64**

One Good Dress **65**

Mackinaw **67**

Yellow **69**

The Stars Cannot Possibly Love You **70**

Ritual **71**

Four Mothers of Demons **72**

Scarecrow **75**

Secrets of the Playground **77**

Three Songs **78**

Mamas Don't Let Your Babies Grow Up in Single-Parent Households **80**

A Good Wife **82**

Untitled II **85**

This Never Gets Any Easier **86**

Impact **87**

Incantation **88**

Eye of the Hummingbird **89**

Ghosts Are Just Strangers Who Know How to Knock **91**

Skeleton Plotting **92**

Nocturne Recall **93**

Sacrament **94**

Small Talk **95**

Coping **96**

Untitled **98**

Burden **101**

Showtime **103**

Me and My Boy **104**

Donor **106**

Service **108**

Bigger **109**

The Wives **110**

Playdate **111**

They Tasted like the Dollar Store Candy I Bought My Son Every Year at Xmas **114**

Cake by the Ocean **115**

baby, baby **116**

Acetone **118**

Road Kill **119**

Hide-and-Seek **121**

Clean **122**

Cosplay **124**

The Smallest Star in the Universe is Meant Only for You **125**

Knock Knock

GHOSTS ARE JUST STRANGERS

SOMEWHERE THERE IS A FIELD WHERE THE BIRDS WILL DIE FOR YOU

I once saw a picture. It was twilight and the grasses in the fields combed themselves towards the gnarled pear trees. The sky did not exist, but the birds did. Their blue wings filled the air. Feathers rocked from the sky and covered the fields in a blanket of indigo. There was no way to know if it was day or night. In the middle of the field stood a man. He stared down at the feathers. He looked tired. I thought of my tiny bedroom in my yellow house. My warm bed. My walls are blue like the feathers. The man in the picture is familiar.

The man comes to visit me at night. He is tired and asks to sleep in my bed. His body is cold as he curls up next to me. He whispers, *the journey is very long to the end of the road.* Outside my little window the birds begin to murmur.

I wake up in the field of feathers. They float up and then down every time I breathe. Standing over me are two young boys. They hold their hats in their hands. Their faces are smeared like drying paint and I cannot make out their features. One boy holds a gun. *We shot the birds from the sky*, the boy says. He points the gun above him, and I see the sun. It ripples its way over the black branches of the trees in waves of orange and yellow. The feathers around me begin to burn. The boys do not move. It is quiet and I hear the sound of footsteps on the road. I hear the sound of the bones in the feathers crunching as they come closer. I know the man is coming for me. He was cold when I left him in my bed.

A SMALL INFESTATION FOLLOWING A BIG STROKE OF LUCK

Mom won a year's supply of Dr Pepper. She earned it. After drinking hundreds of liters, she managed to save every cap, turned them into the address on the label, and won. I came home from school and she was sitting at the kitchen table, blinking at a creased letter in her hands, her mouth a tiny bow of surprise. *I've never won a damn thing in my life, Petey.* She only called me *Petey* if she was happy. Petey was my name between the ages of two and twelve, back when I still ate her thumb-printed PB&J sandwiches. We watched Bugs Bunny together and snorted out our laughs.

Two weeks later, the kitchen was filled with empty soda bottles. They consumed the kitchen table, the countertops, and the dog's water bowl. It had been a week since I had seen Dinty, our dotted terrier. The refrigerator door wouldn't shut. The bottles had taken over and Mom and I couldn't keep up with them. The recycling truck only came once a week. They put a warning note on the big purple bin telling us that we were over our allotted amount. Mom wasn't sure what the allotted amount was. She didn't know what allotted meant either.

I was already sick of the taste of soda, but Mom refused to stop drinking Dr Pepper. She told me if she stopped, they would just send more to make up for the fact that she wasn't drinking enough. I imagined her on an assembly line in a soda factory, grabbing each bottle's neck as it sped by, gulping the fizzing brown liquid. The conveyor belt picks up speed.

Soda bottles smear past her as she grabs for each one, her hands squeezing air like lemons. Lucille Ball is standing in the background imitating Mom as a laugh track cuts through the air and Lucille's mouth collapses into a pouty vermeil frown.

The delivery man kept coming, like clockwork, every Friday at 2:00 p.m.. There was never enough time to answer the door, so he started piling up the boxes of soda like ancient man-made statues. One day I saw a British Columbian totem pole peeking in, leering at me through the hallway window. I heard Mom call out from somewhere in the back study, but I couldn't be sure. I think she was asking for her monkey slippers.

The bottles reproduced their way into the living room. Their young came in the form of one-liter bottles, flopping and bouncing on the carpet. They formed small piles and helped each other climb onto the couch. One got savvy and learned how to operate the TV remote. Their favorite show was *Bonanza*. They would bump against each other like they were clapping whenever Hoss made a joke.

The bottles and their offspring and their offspring's offspring had filled the entire house. They were like overpopulated birdlife on a minikin island: herding together in patchy groups and making guttural plastic noises with their capless tops. They had popped their caps off two weeks prior like a rite of passage, puffing out their hollowed bodies in a show of bravado.

One month after winning, Mom disappeared. I could barely make it out of my room by then. The house started to smell like the time I left Sugar Daddies in the back seat of Mom's Chevy. By the time we noticed, they had melted together like abstract art—decaying caramel weeping in the sun's slanted grin. There was a dispute between Diet and Regular. They didn't like how their labels were different colors. The bottles started to collapse on each other, swaying and twitching as they squared off, the unchoreographed plastic version of *West Side Story*. I managed to escape out the bathroom window, imagining I was a jet because "When you're a Jet you're a Jet all the way," just as the bottles began their uprising. I crash-landed on my knees and palms, dog paddled in the dirt until I managed to stand and run. I heard Mom scream as the sound of plastic kabooms ruptured the air, like ducks shattering in the sky.

PRAISE THE LORD AND PASS THE AMMUNITION

The women make their pies from scratch. Their hands are cracked and white with the baking flour that settles into the creases of their knuckles. They dip their fingers inside the pie filling, tasting it with the tip of their tongues. Their lips are painted red like the name on their husbands' fighter planes. *Stella Sue.*

For the past five months since their husbands left for war, they have learned to stretch and save, to make every scrap of food last. They know how to render the lard. How to trim the blood spots from the meat. The fat glistens like white gold.

Each of the women prepares coffee early in the morning after their children have left for school. They take care to reuse the coffee grounds. The liquid is black and not a dull brown. It is faded like the roots of their hair.

The women's children press their hands together at suppertime, heads bowed. Their scalps are combed and clean. The women make sure of this. *Praise the Lord and pass the ammunition*, the children recite. Their smiles are innocent when their hands turn into guns. They point and shoot. *You're dead!* they yell.

The women miss their husbands. They eye the young men in the market as they bag their foodstuff. Sometimes they have the young men deliver their groceries to their homes. The women remove their wedding bands from their fingers and leave them on butcher blocks or kitchen windowsills.

They want to feel the young men's skin, smooth as gunmetal, behind closed doors.

When the women gossip it is always about other women. How tight the flag is folded when it is passed to them, so it does not fall apart. They wonder when it will be their turn. They sip their coffee from bone-white teacups, leaving lipstick stains on the edges. Even after scrubbing, the red smear never comes off.

Sometimes the women meet in sitting rooms or at kitchen tables and talk in hushed tones as their children sleep. They reminisce about school dances, football games, high school sweethearts. They rub cold cream on their chapped hands, avoiding each other's eyes. They massage the blisters on their feet, conceal their unkempt toenails. Their hair is tied and swept up in kerchiefs, hiding their rollers. They wonder how long the curls will last the next day. They look outside through kitchen windows, past empty clotheslines, just beyond the town's center. They watch the night sky, uncertain. They watch as the lights from the factory blink a tired Morse code.

I LOST MY ORGASM

Maybe I dropped it as I struggled to hold in my hands the box of Munchkin donuts and the lukewarm cup of coffee that I brought for you. Even after you told me not to. Even after you told me you needed space.

I watch you now, my back barely touching your front door that still hasn't shut all the way, allowing the last of the summer flies to creep in. You grip your phone against the hard line of your mouth, pacing the hallway between your living room and the kitchen like an ensnared animal. I want to look between my feet, by the front door behind my sweating back, because I know it's here somewhere, but I can't take my eyes off you. Even now, as you continue to act like I don't exist, even as you're yelling so loud into your phone *CUSTOMER SERVICE REPRESENTATIVE* that there are specks of spit flying out of your mouth, you still mesmerize me. I hug the donut box closer to my chest, remembering when we used to have sex on your leather couch, our skin sticking together until we collapsed on each other, exhausted, our bodies becoming burdened tree branches after a heavy snowfall. We ordered Chinese and watched the Discovery Channel, documentaries about cruise ships so enormous no dock can hold them. A space inside for cabins the size of houses. A shopping mall and a waterpark amidships. An amusement park with a zoo; rollercoasters and elephants. We laughed, considering how we could live forever on a cruise ship that size, with everything we could ever want, cruising the oceans until there was nowhere left to go.

THINGS THEY DON'T TALK ABOUT IN PARENTING CLASS

You prepare your son's breast milk by heating it gently in the pan of boiling water. The tiny bottle bobs and lulls like a lost buoy, the fawn-colored liquid inside bubbling slow and steady, like waves before they rogue.

You take the bottle out, press the fake nipple against your wrist like you have watched your wife do every day, and test the tepid temperature. You screw the lid off the bottle, hover it over your cup of black coffee, and pour it in. You take a loud sip, relishing the sweet taste of your wife's milk.

She has been ignoring you, your wife. Not on purpose, of course. Lately, all her attention has been directed towards your new son. You understood this was going to happen. The new parenting classes you both took at the hospital advised you of this. A new baby means things change. Still, you miss when your lips once touched the sweet petals of your wife's areolas. How she would tremble like a shy earthquake about to erupt. The power of your touch was always a wonder for you. Now, Vaseline clung to dry, cracked nipples where your mouth once sucked. Her breasts were huge buffalo bladders, swollen with lightning-struck scars on stretched skin.

You hand the bottle with the remaining liquid to your wife. She looks up at you, storm clouds under her eyes, and pushes her lips into a smile. *Daddy's little boy,* she says.

RUNT

In the kitchen, Lloyd is wringing its neck like a wet washcloth. Seconds ago, the cat stood smug on the kitchen counter. It hooked the bacon frying on the stove with its paw, meeting Lloyd's eyes with derision. Lloyd always considered cats to be pretentious. He kept the killing clean, painless.

When he was nine, his father killed their dog with the exactness of a slaughterhouse worker. Tall and husky, he whipped around with the grace of a ballerina, squeezing the dog's throat then snapping its neck. The steak it had stolen from his father's plate hung from its mouth like a limp meat rag. The dog lay between them like a sacrificial offering. Lloyd did not finish his supper that night. At first, he felt disgust—a coil of rancor unraveled in his gut, up his throat. He despised his father's weathered flannel shirts, how he never bothered to scrub the dirt from under his nails, the vein throbbing in his neck. His mother was a cowering animal. She played hide-and-seek with the light, blinking at the sun glaring outside the windows. Lloyd was forgotten, pushed away from her breast the way an animal snubs the runt of the litter. They all lived in separate corners.

Lloyd is massive now, two of his father smashed together. The cat, lifeless, peeks past him with a flaccid, dull look. Pleased, he steps over it and picks the bacon out of the pan, pushing the strips of fat belly into his mouth. His son gapes up at him, two soggy egg-yolk eyes and a picture-perfect O mouth, begging for a piece of the kill. Lloyd wets his lips and finishes the last wave of curling fat, wiping his mouth clean with the back of his grease-smeared hands.

HUCKLEBERRY

You are walking through a forest. It is dusk and you see a field full of wildflowers in the distance. You want to smell the flowers, but a river is blocking your way. The river is not swollen so you decide to cross. When your feet enter the water, you realize the water is hot. You look down and see the river is hot chocolate. Marshmallows bob and mounds of whipped cream become stuck on the sides of your legs. You look up and see a man standing on the other side of the river. He is beckoning to you. He is wearing a black cowboy hat, a black suit, and has a dark swirly mustache. You realize it is Val Kilmer from the movie *Tombstone*. You hear him shouting something, but the river drowns his words. You walk faster and as you do, you reach down to scoop up the marshmallows and eat them. Your mouth is full when you reach Val Kilmer. He looks at you and says, *I'm your Huckleberry*. He starts coughing up blood into his hands. He looks down at the blood and then looks at you. You take a closer look at him and realize he is not Val Kilmer at all but your friend who died years ago. You open your mouth to say what you never had the chance to say but all that comes out is a tiny white cloud.

DEAD BOYS

The last boy who loved me
died three years ago
on a dirty couch
after smoking meth
his dive bar crush left
as a parting kiss.

Is there a way to know
if love-struck boys
turn into smoke
once the high is gone?

A dead boy's lips
won't tell lies,
but they'll hold regret
like a tender bite
from bitter fruit.

I don't mind
kissing mortuary thread
sewn on stiff mouths
to keep their souls safe.

Dead boys
don't leave bruises
that are hard to cover
with makeup and sunglasses.
If we're being honest
they have good reason
for ghosting.

John Lennon said, "Everybody loves you when you're six
foot in the ground." Will anyone love me after I'm burned
to ashes the way fresh snow covers the footprints of last
night's mistakes?

A coroner will tell you
a heart removed
from its body will
beat just long enough
to remember all the times
it had to die.

I know that dead boy loved me,
but I didn't love him,
like Lennon said
until he was burned to ashes.
Maybe he still does.

LOSS AVERSION

I used to bury my mother's lockets in the backyard. Planted peach pits. Nothing ever grew except me and my brother and we outgrew the yard, so we started setting fires in the alleys and breaking into the neighbor's houses, but not to steal. We only rearranged their furniture. I pierced my bellybutton with a safety pin, pushed it halfway through and stopped, lost my virginity in the basement of my dad's house. I almost killed my friend driving too fast on a mountain curve. I never saw the deer crossing the road because I was venting about a boy.

There was always a boy back then wanting me, but not wanting me in the easy teenage way of fucking in other people's basements or cars but never our own. I hid myself in closets, kissed the mouths of other women's boyfriends. I tried to arrange myself in bedrooms, houses, lives I didn't belong in. I am staring at myself in a mirror that doesn't belong to me—I don't recognize myself.

Help me find myself in the harsh needles of the pine trees along Route 36, in the body of a deer still moving on the side of the road, in the fruit left to rot in the alleys, in my mother's rough sketches—see? Her lockets are still buried. Even the red-hot end of the cigarette in my father's mouth still burns my name when it touches my skin and tells me I have found you.

THE DEAD ROOM

In my dream, Larry is dead now. There's a room in a house where I can visit him and the others. The room is carpeted in pinkish beige with stairs that lead to a small, square attic with windows. It's sunny and vacant. The Scottish actor who played a teacher in a tough inner-city high school in an early '90s sitcom is there. He isn't dead. He tells me the room is The Dead Room. I can visit my dead and talk to them, but I can't stay, no matter how much I want to. There's music playing but I can't tell what it is. Once, I heard a song and I couldn't get it out of my head. I never found out who sang it. I only know I want to hear it over and over again. I visit Larry and ask him when it happened. He can't talk, of course, but I get the feeling it's been years. Where was I? I can't remember time anymore since Pete died. My dead are growing restless and they need me to leave. The sun is shifting to shades of deep purple while the carpet glows red. I don't want to leave, but I do. The Scottish actor appears and says to me, *It's easier to talk to the dead than the living, isn't it?*

Last night I heard music playing. It was so close in the black bedroom, but I couldn't make out the words.

BOTTLE ROCKETS

Ryan Gardino wants to go down on you. He tells you this over the phone while you're halfway on and halfway off the couch in your basement, nervously wrapping the faded yellow telephone cord around your left ankle, then your right ankle, and now you can't move.

While your dad is working late and your brother is setting off bottle rockets at the neighbor's house two blocks down, Ryan Gardino shows up on your doorstep. He's two years older than you, in the tenth grade, and has a Mohawk. Your hand is stuck to the latch on the screen door as you watch him take a long, relaxed drag off his cigarette and toss it into the flowerpot next to the door.

You let him inside, and as he passes you, his leather jacket jingles from the small chains and music band buttons pinned on like war badges. He smells like leather and nicotine. His slow spreading grin stops midway as he asks if anyone else is home. You tell him you're alone, but your brother might be home soon. Last week you acted out the entire movie of *The Princess Bride* with your best friend. You talked all night, fashion magazines spread out like a picnic blanket, and wondered why the girls in your class smeared makeup on and wore Victoria's Secret bras. You're scared shitless of the boys in your class. They walk down the halls in noisy packs, laughing and punching each other, smelling like gym class and cologne.

Ryan's fingers are tapping on the small of your back like a piano as you lead him into your room. You see it through his eyes: puffy pillows, a daybed with a rose comforter, your favorite stuffed horse your dad won at the school carnival in fifth grade. Clothes shoved and half hanging like tiny cloth bird wings out of your dresser drawer. He walks over to your stereo and flips the switch on, turning the music up as he slides out of his jacket like a snake shedding its skin while staring at you. He has a sideways smirk on his face as he approaches you, hands out, not playing the keyboard of your back any more but still ready to touch you. When he does— touch you—your stomach—already in painful knots—flips and seizes. Your heart is a dying bird in flight. He takes your hand and leads you to your daybed. You see your stuffed bear, Mr. Noodles, shoved between the wall and bed frame, gaping at you with a look of abandonment. Before childhood guilt can creep in, you are falling backwards on your bed as he lands on top of you, his mouth on your neck, sucking, leaving hickies—you're almost positive—that you will have to cover up with makeup you don't yet own. There's an oven in between your legs, gobbling its way up until it reaches your throat. You're thinking about how people kiss in the movies and trying to imitate them, but your tongue keeps hitting his and you stifle your giggles.

Your room faces the baseball field and you can hear the neighbor's boys shouting and the sound of the steel bats as they hit the ground. You try to remember what first base and second base are as he smuggles his hand inside your bra, groping your A-cup breasts that are still in the process of shaping themselves, still growing into their full potential. He plays with your nipples like they're pegs on a Battleship game board. You swore to your best friend to never let a boy go up your shirt, to never be like the other girls in your class. Now, a boy is panting on you like a heat-exhausted dog and his crotch is a steel poker in between your legs. There are ten of him, all doing different things, and you can't keep track, and you feel like one of your brother's bottle rockets, dizzy as you launch into the sky, exploding into a thousand pieces. This isn't how you imagined it. Your mouth is covered with his mouth and his fingers are unbuttoning your pants, sliding each pant leg down to your ankles, and his hands are giant spiders inside your pink polka dot panties.

You think about your mom and all the men she brought home over the years, how fast she could switch from yelling at you and your brother to laughing at everything when a man showed up at the door, flirting in the kitchen like you weren't there, like you didn't exist. But you were there, standing in the corner in a pink nightgown, holding your glass of chocolate milk. The distant sound of bottle rockets shooting off fills your room as it slowly fades into a dirty yellow haze. Your hands find their way on either side of his shaved head. You cautiously rub the stubble surrounding his Mohawk, not knowing if this is right or wrong, if this is where it all starts, or how it is supposed to start. You think you need to listen to your brother and just shut up and grow up. Ryan Gardino's head is moving down now, his Mohawk like the fin of a shark as he drags his tongue past your belly button, blazing a trail like Red Hots candies down, further down, and somewhere in the background you can hear Fugazi singing: "You can't be what you were, so you better start being just what you are."

THE DIFFERENCE BETWEEN A RAVEN AND A CROW

I am dreaming of floods again and wildfires; too many omens have been ignored. *The Farmers' Almanac* is always right. It tells me how farmers believed there would be no rain until the fields were burned to the ground. It tells me the difference between a raven and a crow is ravens always travel in pairs. Farmers can't speak of the storms in my heart. I never told my father I can sense a person's death. I am relieved when the neighbor dies in his sleep. His heart gave out before the fire ate its way into his house. My father took me camping when I was ten. Before we could pitch our tent, the wind kicked up and rain came down, hard as fists. I watched our tent blow away while my father gave chase towards the swollen river. I saw a fawn struggling in the rapids as a doe paced the riverbank. My father let our tent blow by him as he sized up the whitewater, contemplating the jump. Today I fell asleep on the bus again. A baby's screams woke me as rain pelted the windows and doors. The night my grandmother died I hit a raven head-on with my car. I can smell the wildfires coming despite the rain. I can feel someone is drowning but all I see are the crows outside my window.

LULLABY

Remember what your mother told you. Take your plain pink panties off and put on the lace thong—yes, the one with the red bow. Speaking of red, smear the tube of red on your lips, make them pop. Smack your lips together a few times. Spray the body perfume you bought from Victoria's Secret and walk into it. Spray, walk. You smell like hot candy. You look like cool heat. You hit the sidewalk like a suit on Wall Street. Approach the car window and lean in, but not too far. Squeeze your elbows into your waist; your tits look bigger when you do this. Say something clever. Don't sound too dumb, don't sound too smart. Name your price. Stick to it. Don't break eye contact. When the car door opens, slide inside, your skin sticking to the hot polyester like a Band-Aid. Stay cool when his hand grabs your knee. Smile big. Show your teeth. When he starts to drive make sure to keep track of the scenery passing by. He doesn't tell you his name, but he asks for yours. Tell him your name is Candy. Smile again when he licks his lips. Act like you enjoy his hand running up your skirt. Feel your smile start to fade when he pulls over and reaches behind him, shows you the coil of rope and grins. When he grabs you before you can move, before you can scream, try to remember where the door handle is. When he binds your hands together and points the gun at your head, nod when he asks if you're going to be a good girl. When he turns on the radio and "Sittin' on the Dock of the Bay" comes on, try not to cry, because that's your mother's favorite song. Remember when she sang it to you at bedtime when you were a girl. Remember her face, beautiful and calm as you slipped into your dreams. Say goodbye to the city. Say hello to cornfields, to the lake stretched out before you like a hunter's skinned trophy. Notice how even the birds have stopped their chatter to watch you. Try to find the weak spot in the rope binding your wrists together. Bite his hand when he leans towards you. Don't cry when he slaps you and calls you a whore. You're a good girl. Breathe through your nose when the duct tape forces your lips shut. Don't look at the gun in his hand. When he carries you to the lake keep your eyes on the sky. Hit the water like a broken bird. The water melts over you like a second skin. Recognize the moment when you stop trying to fight. How the air becomes concrete in your lungs. Try to remember what your mother told you. Her face, sinking like you are now, the water heavy as syrup as it rocks you to sleep.

HOLES

With Attribution to Leonora Desar

They lay down on the bed, his head inside her chest. He thinks of how a heart is like an engine, if the oil runs out it will seize. He saw a broken engine at his mechanic's shop once, right after their daughter Lily disappeared. *See that?* The mechanic said, pointing a socket wrench at the hole. *If you don't check your oil, that's going to be your engine.* That's going to be his heart. Too many cigarettes, too much booze, and love tethered then clipped. She slips him inside of her, asks if he wants it faster. He answers in heavy breaths. When the shaking subsides, she doesn't touch him. They fall asleep and wake to an Amber Alert on his phone, flashing like a neon sign. He shuts his eyes and dreams of a little girl stolen. The girl is in a car with a man speeding down a curling highway. The trees lean in on either side of the road, straining to see inside. The man tells the girl the engine sounds funny, and if she isn't careful, he'll bust a hole right through her heart. He hands her a gallon of strawberry milk and she drowns herself in pink, erasing her face. The man whistles to the music on the radio as he drives, the trees in the rearview mirror folding like two dark wings.

When he wakes up, the dog outside is barking, the coffee machine is grumbling, and she's gone, a hole on the side of the bed where her body used to be.

HIS BONES

From the moment she pushed her son out of her body, she knew she had to protect him. From the pain of his father leaving. From the blood he left behind. Her son screamed, fierce and proud. Her heart bruised after years of misuse.

When he grew into a child he fell and broke his arm. The doctors placed a cast around the broken limb. His classmates colored their names: *Get well! Lorenzo, Max, Tanisha.* The bone healed in time, on its own, as most things do. She read that all bones start as cartilage. Eventually it hardens, both inside and out, until it completes its transformation in adulthood. She watched as her son's arms and legs began to stretch like a canvas. His limbs were the painted trees in the woods behind their cabin, always reaching for something she couldn't see. But he could. She taught him the love of the forest, the smell of the earth. She gathered the soil around them as a blanket on cold nights. The warmth of their ancestors, gone for centuries but always near, their souls filling in the gaps of night.

A year after her son went missing in the woods, the sheriff told her his remains would never be found. She ran through the forest searching, smelling him everywhere. He was the wind now, the roots of the trees. The animals she once loved and protected she now hated. They stole his remains. His bones were not meant for them. It was the way of nature, she read, for animals to scavenge. Every time she looked for him, her heart calcified into a knot. She screamed at the foxes and wolves, her lips revealing her own vicious snarl. They feared her hunger as it hung in their air and filled the spaces between the trees.

When the sheriff called, she was told to meet him at the coroner's office. She walked into a room with a metal table and stared at the pile of dirty white bones that was once her son. She touched as many pieces as she could, feeling the grooves where the teeth from the animals had left their final marks. She would return his bones to the forest that night and disappear in the comfort of the trees and earth. The animals would take her down, and she wouldn't fight them.

SUPERTRAMP

They are waiting for you to make your way home. The sun is dying outside. You write a letter and leave it for your family. You write what you know about happiness and sign your real name. Flashes of red and orange flood the window of the abandoned bus like a finale of fireworks. The bus you have called home for months. You remember being happy as a kid, face smeared with chocolate, body warm from your mother's kisses. Feel that again. Four years old, walking out of your house at two in the morning. Found in Mrs. Fischer's kitchen eating her secret stash of Halloween candy. Your parents hugged you until you couldn't breathe. Your mother said your soul never sat still.

The strength to find a path across the river is missing. You smell of death, decay. Your hunger is the grizzly that walked past you, no longer recognizing you as food. Your face, the skeleton of the moose you killed. The moose you wasted, not knowing how to skin it. How to keep the maggots away. *The worst tragedy of my life*. The belt no longer holds your pants against your thinning waist, even with the extra holes you carved. Home, a bittersweet taste. The berries you ate, thinking they were edible. You are starving inside a mistake you cannot change. You think of your trip north and the people you met. People that became your friends. Friends you wished were your family, but you still left them behind. They call you *Supertramp*. People up north say spring is the cruelest season. Spring has wrapped a noose around your neck. The moment you graduated from college you cashed out your savings and nosed your old Datsun towards the mountains. A compass magnet drawing north, the pull like the river's rapids that trap you here in this bus you call home. Someone will find you after you are gone.

Write the letter you have been unable to write until now.

SABA ON THE SHOF

For the past three weeks, he has done everything he can to distract himself. Today, he decides to take a walk down to the beach. He holds Rivka's letter like an injured bird. The crease where he folded the paper into a square is two days old. It is too late to make it smooth again.

The waves are frantic that morning, frothing and leaving suds on the shoreline. He sits down in one of the white plastic chairs left in the sand, his bones an old ship, creaking. How many days has his grandson, Naftali, been held hostage? He has shied away from the news, locked himself inside his room. He counts his coins, prays, stares at the beach, hoping to see a young man with light in his hair.

When his son died, Rivka was left to raise Naftali on her own. He was a beautiful boy who looked like he swallowed the sun. Naftali's face lit up whenever he saw him. *Saba!* he would shout, running—always running—towards him. *Cover my eyes and spin me until I'm dizzy!* He did his best to be a father figure to his grandson. Even so, Naftali was as untamed as the waves hitting the shore in front of his chair. The city was dangerous but alluring to a young man. Rivka could never keep him under her thumb.

He feels the edges of the letter with his finger, touching what is written on the paper from Rivka. She told him she would write when they found Naftali. If he was alive, she would send a car for him. The car never came, but the letter did. Even the softest touch, Saba knows, cannot make the words it contains less cutting. He covers the letter with both of his palms, as if he is praying, and stares at the water. How long can a man hide? How long he can hide here, on this shore? When Naftali was still a boy, he would ask questions. *Why do the birds sing, Saba? Is the sun always yellow?* One night, after Rivka went to bed, Naftali asked him quietly: *How long until I become a man?* Saba stares at the waves, gripping the letter, remembering his reply: *Sometimes in the blink of an eye.*

THE OCEAN RESONATES IN EMPTY SPACES

For Cobain

I knew I would make you out of shining strands of hair and the smooth shells I collected that day on the beach. They were pink and soft like the inside of a baby's ear. There were too many shells to pick from, so I carried all of them home with me. The weight of the shells damaged my hands and I could not piece you perfectly together. You stood in front of me and wobbled. You reached out to touch me, but I could not touch you back with my fractured hands. You started to cry but instead of tears I heard the ocean. I reached out my arms to you while my hands dangled like two broken birds from my wrists.

Ours is just a little sorrow, I said.

PALADIN

Sometimes, in a twenty-four hour diner in Beaumont, Texas, you'll find Buck pouring coffee into lemon-colored mugs. Maybe the steam hits his hardened face long enough to make him appear young again. Homeless teens calling themselves *Regulators* burst in at two in the morning, scattering coins and demanding coffee and pie. *This is America,* they tell Buck. He thinks about how unforgiving the sun was when he was twelve. It doesn't matter; he knows things have a way of dying when they are forgotten. The leaves building up in his granddaddy's backyard gather into tiny burial mounds scattered across the lawn. His granddaddy is all he has left, so Buck buys a rake. He does the yardwork without complaint. Sometimes, when Buck rakes, he hums "The Ballad of Paladin." His father used to sing this while cleaning his gun, peering at him through the empty barrel. His eye seemed very far away. The leaves in Buck's granddaddy's yard huddle close, forming their game plan, and Buck thinks: a storm is scraping itself together. *Have gun will travel* (rake) *a knight without armor* (scrape) *Paladin, Paladin, where do you roam?* Buck sees himself and what is now his life in the grease that builds up on the diner's crusted grill. In the pink of the chewing gum that collects under the stools at the counter after the bar crowd stumbles back home, wherever home is. There are times when the smoke from the grease is so thick he can't escape. He moves around the diner like a drunken chess piece, unable to find a pocket of air worth breathing. Years ago, his wife staggered inside, polka dots of blood painting the outside of her nostrils. She collapsed in the stall of the bathroom while foamy white clouds oozed between her blue lips. Buck returned to the diner the day after Patty was buried. He walked back to the women's restroom, opened the stall, and stared hard at the toilet. Stared hard at the walls of the stall. They were an angry yellow. It burned Buck's eyes. He took a black magic marker out of his pants pocket and leaned in, remembering how his wife's hair was the color of the sun in an empty sky. He scrawled on the wall of the stall in loopy cursive: *Far, far from home.*

YOU CAN ALWAYS COME BACK

My best friend growing up was a boy named Seth who lived across the street from me. We were both in the same kindergarten class and hung out after school every day. Seth was allergic to dairy and had to eat his cereal with water. Seth liked to wear plaid shirts. Seth would push me on the swings on the playground. According to our classmates, Seth and I were going to get married when we grew up. It was only after he moved away and over twenty years had passed did I think to start searching for him.

It was Thanksgiving in 2008 when I started looking for Seth online. Instead of finding him on Facebook or Instagram, I found his obituary. He died seven months prior. I also discovered his ex-wife, who emailed me that Seth died alone in his bathtub from an accidental drug overdose. I knew immediately why, or at least what the obvious reason would be. When Seth was five, he almost died after being hit by another car while his mom was driving him to school. The aftermath was a lifelong demon that would follow him until his death twenty-five years later.

I remember waking up one morning after the accident and walking across the street to play with Seth. There was a moving truck parked outside his family's house and workers loading all of their possessions into the back of it, but his dad's belongings weren't included. His parents were getting a divorce. It might have been because of the accident, or the trauma that followed, or both. The entire left side of Seth's body had been paralyzed. He couldn't run, but he could do a kind of half-run half-scrape jog. He couldn't push me on the swings with both hands, so he used his right one. We adjusted. Little kids are good at that. They're adaptable.

I stood in my mom's kitchen the morning I found the obituary and told her Seth was dead. *Hmm?* She said, opening the door to the oven to peer at the crisping lump of meat inside. *Seth's dead.* I repeated. She turned around and saw the look on my face. *Elizabeth's son? Oh, that's too bad.* She opened the oven door again and poked. *They were such a great family.* Her friendship with Seth's mom had been deeper than the typical neighborly, our-kids-play-together way. They would sit on Seth's back porch and smoke cigarettes, whispering and laughing while we played upstairs. I touched the potatoes resting on the counter that were ready to be skinned and boiled and watched as they wobbled away from me. I wanted to hear more. I wanted her to tell me stories I didn't remember about Seth. I wanted to her to explain why Seth left and came back someone different. Why his dad left and never came back, leaving Seth's mom no choice but to move. I wanted to tell her about the time he slammed his thumb in the door of his bedroom, or how I would make faces at him while he ate his cereal with water instead of milk. *What happens if you're allergic to milk and you drink it?* I asked him. *Do you die? Almost,* he said. *But you can always come back. It's like being halfway dead.*

There are lots of ways to remain half alive and half dead. Tons.

After that Thanksgiving dinner, I went home and wrote Seth a letter. My boyfriend at the time told me it would be a good idea to find closure. Months before, he'd moved halfway across the country to attend his MFA program. By the time he left, I barely recognized him. He was different from the night of our first date. So was I. We spent the night in Cap Hill for Halloween roaming from one bar to another while zombies and superheroes swept the streets until dawn. Maybe he wanted the letter to be practice for when our relationship finally fell apart two years after he left for grad school. Maybe he wanted me to finally get out all the reasons I regret giving us a second, third, or fourth chance when we never should have survived past our first week of dating. I was a single mom with a baby, while he was working on his undergrad degree in a city an hour away. We were oil and water, at best. My world was unpredictable and filled with temper tantrums, potty training, and dealing with an abusive biological father who wanted custody.

When I wrote the letter to Seth, I was hoping to feel relief from the regret I felt for not finding him sooner. Maybe I was also feeling regret from not trying harder with my relationship. But regret, even if it's leftover regret, still must be dealt with. Even if I'd managed to find Seth before he died, that doesn't mean I could have saved him. And I sure as shit didn't feel any better after writing that letter to him. It's filled with my own guilt. I don't even remember exactly what it says. Maybe it's a thank you to Seth. Maybe it's an apology letter, a series of I'm sorrys and memories of our friendship that ended one day when the leaves were turning from soft to stiff. That letter is stored away in a shoebox in my closet with the name *Seth* on it, sealed. I'll probably never open it.

I didn't realize friendship was something you could physically lose until after Seth's accident. I remember running to his house to escape while my mom and dad fought. His room was warm and smelled like Play-Doh and laundry softener. His bed was filled with alligator and shark stuffed animals and clothing discarded from days before. The neighborhood we lived in wasn't what you see now, a lot of cookie-cutter houses that all look and feel the same. A kind of numbness-box where individuality and creativity aren't allowed. I remember when the hail came down hard one day and broke almost every window in our house, leaving chunks of ice and standing water. It triggered a storm that would eventually end my parents' marriage.

My mother drove back home to Indiana one night and didn't come back for what seemed like weeks. One evening she kissed me goodnight, and the next morning she was gone. My dad walked around with a tight mouth, not giving me or my brother any reason why. When she did come home, she had a giant stuffed dog for me. She held it out in front of her, and the space between me and her and that dog were all the miles she traveled to leave us. But she came back.

They found Seth dead in his bathtub when he didn't show up for work. Not halfway dead. And he didn't come back. No one should die alone, and certainly not in a bathtub. The places we die are sometimes the same places we sought out trying to find some semblance of relief.

I've lived long enough to realize the things that seem like they are coincidences really aren't. Some people will come into your life and stay, and others will leave. Either in the middle of the night after tucking you into bed, or on an airplane on their way to an MFA, or in a car on the way to school. And if they do come back, they aren't the same people they were when they left.

I don't know if Seth remembered what happened after he woke up from his coma in a hospital bed. He left for school that morning one person and woke up in a different body, a body he had to live with until the day he managed to climb into his bathtub with one paralyzed hand and arm and leg and never woke up.

I still have our kindergarten class picture. Seth is sitting cross-legged in the front row, hunched over and barely smiling, wearing a plaid shirt. At some point, I took a pen and marked an X over him along with several other of my classmates. At some point I must have been mad at him enough to want to never see his face again, maybe a childish argument. But I can't remember why. There's another image in my head of Seth on the playground swings at our school. The sun is shining on his hair. His eyes are squinting in that half-awake, half sleepy way they always did. He's missing two of his top front teeth. I can see the man he was supposed to be; a kind of mashed together version of his dad and mom mixed with early '80s movies actors. But I'll never really know. I only have his senior year picture I found online, looking the same as he did then, but not quite an adult and no longer a little boy.

Maybe I chose to look for Seth at the exact moment I knew my relationship was ending as a way to find closure. Discovering Seth was dead in the heart of my unraveling relationship didn't give me any type of direction to be able to make sense of either one. That's what the letter was about. And thinking back now, maybe I wrote the letter more for myself than the person it addressed. That's the thing about people leaving, it doesn't always mean they're gone forever; and death doesn't always mean someone has left. Sometimes absence takes the place of something that was there a long time ago that you can never, ever get back.

WILD HARES

The girls never kissed the boys. The boys that walked down the hallway in packs, smelling of Cheetos and drugstore cologne. The girls never went to school dances, out to movies or late-night pizza. They never wore jewelry. Never a spot of makeup; their skin was fresh like new snow. If their mama caught them trying on her church heels, they were beaten. They never showered with the other girls in gym class, but they caught glimpses of their breasts. How their nipples were small and pink, unlike their own. They wore plain dresses in forgettable colors: beige, olive, navy. Their hair pulled back into a bun. Tight. Uncomplicated. The girls sang in the church choir, cooked suppers for the nursing home folks, babysat Pastor Daniel's kids. Their papa expected them home before the five o'clock news and to have their homework done by the time the weather forecast came on. One Friday their parents left them by themselves overnight. The girls loosened their hair and snuck out the window, scampering down the hill to the abandoned house. The contents of a bottle of Boone's Farm sloshed in one girl's pocket; in another girl's pocket was a pack of stale cigarettes. The girls never noticed Charlie Crick—the man who lived down the alley—following close behind, his breath smelling like the gin mill, his face red and burning. He found the girls inside the empty living room of old Doc Murphy's house. They were passing the bottle of Boone's between them, taking swigs and puffing on a half-lit cigarette. He told each girl to get undressed and not to look as he took them, one by one. He told the jury a month later the girls never opened their eyes, but they must have known. Some of them bled and some of them didn't.

BANG, SNAP!

My hand is digging down the front of your pants like the neighbor's puppy in Mama's flower garden. My other hand is wrapped around yours as you push the barrel of Papa's pistol against my sweaty cheekbone. It's cold and hard, just like our resolution. Two hours ago, we skipped out on forty-one bucks in gas and a bottle of soda pop at the Stop and Slurp off Highway 7. It's the only road that gets you into this shithole town and it's the only road that gets you out. We wanted to go where no one knew us, where no one would ever know our story.

We left this morning, after all the other kids scattered to first period and the blacktop was deserted. I traced a heart in the gravel alongside the basketball court with the tip of my pink jellies and waited for you, the sun a tarnished bottle cap in the sky. My backpack full of clothes and my stuffed unicorn. I chewed my bubble gum, anxious, snapping it with my teeth, the sound reminding me of the Bang Snaps the kids on the block would buy at the fireworks stand for the Fourth of July. We'd throw them down on the ground as hard as we could and wince, waiting for the noise, waiting for the puffs of smoke. *BANG, SNAP!*

My folks never seemed to pay any mind to me when it was Fourth of July. My little brother Joey always wet himself because he was scared of the fireworks. Mama would stay inside the living room to chat with the other women while Papa sat in a busted lawn chair in the driveway; his legs sprawled out like a broken doll. He'd pass you a beer from the ice bucket sitting in between your chair and his. You talked about your high school days with Papa playing football while he reached further down into the ice bucket, his hands shaking as he fished out another beer.

Your eyes began to follow me right around the time I could rest Joey on my curving hip, when it started to hurt my breasts if he clung to me too tightly. I knew you as Uncle Chris, Papa's best friend since grade school. Our secret rendezvous—that's what you called them—became routine after the bell rang at school. You waited around the corner in your Chevy until I came running out to find you, my breath catching in my throat. We've been stuck together like super glue ever since.

Papa came looking after I didn't show up for fourth period and he brought the police along with him. You tell me they have your truck out on the APB and skipping out on that gas probably didn't help any. I can still see Mama in the crowd of dark blue uniforms. Her mascara is streaking down her face like two exhausted storm clouds. The police are surrounding our truck, guns pointing straight and steady like a hunting dog's snout caught on a scent. A voice is pleading through a megaphone to put the gun down. It sounds like Papa when he's been drinking too much—what Mama calls his whiskey voice. I feel like someone stole my last good breath.

I think about the farm—the land out back of my bedroom window the morning after it snows. A million crystals embroidering the yard like one of Mama's quilts. How it burns my eyes to look at them all at once. I want to crawl into my bed and pull the covers over me so no one can see me. I want to hug Mama and say goodbye to Joey. I want to tell Papa that I'm sorry. I need to tell him I'm still his little girl, but sometimes true love finds you in the emptiest of places.

The police keep looking at you and then at me and they're motioning with their arms. They're gonna take you away and lock you up, just like you said. We'll never see each other again. I think of your hands touching me, weightless, like aged silk slipping across my body. You nod your head and I do the same.

Fireworks are in your eyes as you kiss me, your lips hot metal and tasting like cigarettes. You taste like the home we will never have. You pull away from me and your hands aren't shaking at all as you push Papa's pistol against my forehead. I squeeze my eyes shut. I am squeezing them so hard that all I see is white. I am listening. I am listening and I am waiting for the noise.

FINAL TRUMPET

When I think I am far enough away I find a rock and sit. The hill is across from another hill which is across from a mountain. Let me tell you, mountains are everywhere here. Let me tell you something else, there are just as many churches as mountains. From where I sit on my rock, catching my breath, I can hear the pack coming from the west. West is where the tallest peak overlooks the city. Aside from hills and mountains I can also see my house, far away, a tiny dot among rows of multi-colored rows. I know my father is at work. His bright orange Scout is missing from the driveway. I can hear voices bouncing off the hills. It's hard to tell which direction. Maybe they are heading back towards my school.

I want to be safe in my room. I'm fourteen—a kid for fuck's sake. Touching myself is not allowed. So, I touch others. I think my mother always knew. While I knelt, she prayed fervently over me and my father laid his hands on my head. I could feel them shaking. They repeated prayers over and over, their breath smelling of church mints. Over the sound of their voices I could hear the neighbor's daughter playing her trumpet. She was first chair. She made apple pie from scratch. She smelled like wilted roses. The stained-glass window in the hallway leading to her bedroom colored me in all the hues of late fall. The aspen leaves were changing from gold to red to rust. The kind of colors that signaled the leaves would soon begin to crisp and drop. I have never been more aware of the call of the final trumpet. How loud a crack can sound in a small room filled only with the light of late afternoon and a girl removing her peach-colored dress. Of the sound of voices coming up over the hillside as I sit on my rock singing *O death, where is your victory, O death, where is your sting?*

LIFESPAN

On Sunday everyone goes to the Natural History Museum. In the museum is a botanic garden. Butterflies, caterpillars, moths, fauna and flora.

As you step inside the garden you see a little girl with her mother. The girl is holding a butterfly between her chubby fingers. Its wings are a color you have never seen before. The mother looks at you. She pushes her index finger against her lips and says *shhh*. The girl squeezes the butterfly between her fingers. Its wings pulse in unison with your heartbeat. It is the sound of velvet being crushed.

Outside the sun drops from the sky.

I ANSWER THE MISSED CONNECTIONS ON CRAIGSLIST BECAUSE I DON'T WANT PEOPLE TO FEEL ALONE AND I DON'T WANT TO FEEL ALONE EITHER

You smelled like wet grass on a hot day. No one famous died that day. I want to see you sitting on my small couch holding a large glass of wine. Do you like birds? I don't have a hummingbird feeder, but there are hummingbirds outside my window. I want to paint your toenails Mario Bros. Red and Candy Heart Pink. I collect snow globes from airports. I don't own Michigan yet. When I was a kid, I wore my older brother's hand-me-downs. I don't feel like I fit into my own skin. I want to touch someone other than myself. I want your nails to stitch across my skin. Leave beads of blood across my tattoos. After picking the wings off a bee. It still moves.

EXAMINATION

Mallory's gynecologist tells her that she's going to paint her cervix. She says it offhandedly, like she's planning on getting her nails done or run to the grocery store for more milk.

Mallory lies on the exam table, legs spread wide open, thinking about how the rainbow lasagna with heirloom tomatoes will be perfect for Saturday night's dinner with her husband's boss and his wife. Moments earlier, while sitting in Dr. Green's waiting room, she tore out the recipe from the latest issue of *Food & Wine* magazine. Brent, Dan's boss, loves anything she prepares. His wife, Stella, is an east coast snob who doesn't believe in cooking. She only believes in Guillermo, her twenty-four-year-old personal chef. She loves to parade him around the dining room table during dinner parties, running her fingers up and down his chest like she's playing the piano.

Gee-air-mo, Stella says, *is from Brazil. We found him while vacationing in Rio.* Mallory once asked Dan about Guillermo, what he thought Brent felt about Stella flaunting him in his face.

He doesn't seem to mind, Dan told her, hunching over his laptop and squinting his eyes in a way she secretly hated. *He probably has something on the side himself.* Mallory pretended to read her book, but she couldn't help the smile that spread across her face when Brent's name was mentioned. It was easy to remember the way his hand had touched the small of her back in the corner of the kitchen where no one could see them.

This is her third visit this year to Dr. Green, who insists that Mallory call her *Bev*. Since her last two pap smears came back abnormal, Mallory finds herself in metal stirrups every three months for an exam. She keeps a close eye on her cervix like a mother keeps an eye on her toddler. The smell of iodine monopolizes the room and she swears she hears Bev humming "Piano Man." She recalls this time last year, thinking about her vagina the same way she did when she was a teenager: as a throbbing insatiable being. Now, it is home to metal speculums and Bev's gloved fingers.

Alright, Mallory. Now we send this off to the lab to see if there are any abnormal cells.

Mallory likes how Bev says we, as if they are both participating in a project, like scouting for whales from the deck of a cruise ship, index fingers rigidly pointing in the air like hunting dogs' snouts. *Look, there's a gray humpback at two o'clock.*

Bev finishes, pops her latex gloves off with a magician's showmanship, and swivels in her stool to look at her.

This may be a case of HPV versus precancerous cells.

HPV? Mallory vaguely remembers a vaccine commercial which stated 99% of the population has HPV and how men are usually the carriers.

Many people have it and just don't know. Bev's tone is reassuring. *Sometimes, Mallory, it likes to rear its ugly head in times of stress.*

Lately, Mallory's under a blanket of stress that she can't seem to crawl out from under. Dan was spending more and more time away on business, which meant Brent had to oversee him. She couldn't help but feel guilty about how much she misses Brent over her own husband.

Bev stares at her, appearing small and pale in her pink doctor's coat in comparison to Mallory, who decided to wear her royal blue silk blouse Dan bought her for Christmas last year. She looks down at her feet, noticed her French pedicure, propped up as if on display in two metal stirrups. It's starting to chip. Mallory breaks the gaze first, looking over at a poster of an anatomical drawing of a vagina, complete with definitions of each part. The clitoris looks suspiciously small to be drawn to scale. The vagina on the wall reminds her of a story she heard in a class during her undergrad studies.

That drawing on the wall reminds me of a story I heard in college . . . I was a history major. Dan convinced me I was being impractical, so I switched to business management.

Don't you teach yoga? Bev asked, scribbling something on her clipboard.

Well, yes. But before switching majors, I took a medieval studies class. During those times, if a woman was caught committing adultery, their nose and ears were cut off and they were forced to parade their shame to the entire village. Everyone saw which part was responsible for her mutilated face. A cut-off nose resembles a, well, you know.

A vajayjay? Bev asks, clicking her pen. Mallory raises her eyebrows while Bev shrugs. *That's what Oprah calls a vagina.*

I don't have cable.

Listen to me, Mallory, Bev's tone switches like gears in an engine. *You shouldn't have anything to worry about. I've been treating you for over a year now and the probability of having to remove your entire cervix is slim.* She puts her glasses back on and stands, peering down at Mallory with watery, dark eyes.

Rest assured, we will resolve this so that you and Dan can try to start a family, if that's what you still want to do.

Mallory thinks about her husband. The more hours he spends at work, the more they seem to talk about starting a family, as if a baby can fill the gaping hole that has become their marriage. Dan has no idea how she spends her time. How she started playing golf five months ago, or how she volunteers at the women's shelter off the turnpike, which Dan calls *the seedy part of town*. He sounded like such a prick when he said *seedy*. He doesn't know about the nights she claimed to be out with friends while he was working late, about how she was really spending nights wrapped in the blanket of another man. She doesn't know how to tell Dan she doesn't want to start a family, hell, doesn't even want to be a mother. The guilt of what she'd thought was selfishness had been chasing her all year, until she found herself attracted to Brent, Dan's boss. The way he smiled at her during dinner parties or company picnics. She started finding excuses to talk to him away from Dan and Stella. As the months went on, Mallory found herself giving in to Brent's flirtations, which she initially thought was harmless. Until the night they found themselves alone at a company retreat in the mountains. Dan had promised to unbury himself from work but never left his room. Stella hated company retreats and had declined to come.

Bev doesn't wait for confirmation as she gently pats Mallory's hand and leaves the room, the door clicking quietly behind her.

Mallory doesn't move from the exam table. The paper cloth draped across her lap crinkles each time she takes a breath. The metal speculum sits on the counter like a cold art display, and as she stares at the vagina on the wall, the coldness still invading her from the examination, Mallory knows it's time to leave.

ROCKABYE SWEET BABY JAMES

For Mama

When I decided to leave, I gave away all my childhood belongings. I missed the miniature glass animals. I missed the glass horse most. *I understand,* you said. You smashed all your teeth with a small gold hammer and collected the dust in your hands. You melted the dust with a cigarette lighter and made the shape of a small white horse. *Here,* you tried to say, but I couldn't understand you with all your teeth missing. The horse fell from your hands and trotted across the floor before I could grab it. We watched as a tiny cowboy grabbed its mane and climbed on its back. They galloped under the door and into the field behind the house until the sunflowers swallowed him.

Goodnight you moonlight ladies, you sang.

NORTHERN LIGHTS

I was left under a rock in the woods when I was a baby. An older man, his wife, and his son were hiking when they heard me crying. My dad lifted the rock and there I was, cocooned in a cavity of earth. They took pity and brought me home.

When I was five, orange lava flowed across our floor. I jumped from pillow cushion to pillow cushion, hoping my feet wouldn't melt. My brother told me if even one tiny toe touched the lava I would explode. He scrunched his eyebrows in a way that looked serious. I knew he had to be telling me the truth. It took me an hour to get to my bedroom.

When I was seven, my brother broke my favorite Ronald McDonald record. He told me if the album is played backwards, Ronald commands you in a deep, demonic voice to kill your mom and dad. He said he would not tell Mom that my Ronald McDonald album was satanic, or that I was possessed. He said he broke it in half for my own good.

When I was eight, I told my brother I wanted to float like Alice in the scene from *Alice in Wonderland*. He told me to put on my poofiest skirt. He said if I jumped off the top of the stairs I would fly into forever. He tied a rope around my waist just to be safe. Hurry and jump before Mom finds us. Mom came into the kitchen just as I readied myself to leap. She told my brother to go to his room while she untied the rope from my waist, shaking her head. *You always believe the sun rises and sets on your brother.*

When I was twelve, I stood on the grass in our yard, watching my brother fight another boy from school. My brother was big, but this boy was bigger. Their faces signaled red and white and red again. My brother was losing his breath. I ran inside and grabbed the cordless phone. I came outside as the crowd from school formed a ring around the lawn. I shouted that Mom called and was on her way home. Everyone scattered and my brother was left alone on the grass. *I had that kid pinned,* he told me. We both knew better.

When I was twenty-one, I returned home on Christmas day. My brother was staying in the basement. The garage door was pulled down and billowing smoke. It was different than smoke from a fire. It smelled like fumes. I opened the side door into the garage and found my brother inside his car, a bottle of whiskey in his lap and his eyes closed. I couldn't breathe. The exhaust puffed out of the tailpipe like an industrial waste cloud, squeezing my lungs. I opened the car door and dragged my brother out, thinking *hurry* as the whiskey bottle fell and broke in half, thinking *hot lava,* thinking *hurry and jump before Mom comes home.*

When I am thirty-five my brother takes a plane to Alaska and never returns. After three months I follow his trail, searching the national park for signs he is alive. I search for his favorite orange tent, for his hiking backpack with the Maui patch sewn on the back flap, for the abandoned campfire piled with American Spirit Mellow Yellow cigarette butts. The park rangers tell me people go missing every year and are never found. My mom begs me to return home. Losing both her children will kill her. I intended to stay and wait for the northern lights.

One day, the sky glows Christmas green. The park rangers find me on a trail heading south and tell me to return home. I tell them I met a woman in the forest last week with her two young children. She told me to watch the sky, that it would soon be changing colors. She said people call the colors the northern lights, but they are not lights at all. They are the reflections of a fire from the dead letting us know they are thinking of us. They are trying to tell us they are safe, even though we are very far apart.

PEOPLE CALL YOU A SPACE COWBOY

Outside your room I found a record player. It was playing the Jackson Five album you owned when you were five years old. It was stuck on "I'll Be There." When you tried to remove the needle, the door to your room opened. You opened your mouth and the record player began playing your voice:

This is what happens when you place all your faith in the universe.

GHOSTS

When I was a little girl my grandmother told me my stuffed animals came alive at night and tried to eat children's souls. Last week, a box arrived from my mother with old toys from my childhood. Inside the box was a stuffed bear with a gray handlebar mustache. It looked like real hair. I don't remember owning this bear as a child. The bear resembled Wilford Brimley from the oatmeal commercial, so I named it Wilford Brimley. The first night Wilford Brimley was in my room, I woke up and found him staring at me from the top of my dresser. He was holding an empty shot glass in one paw and a cigarette stub burned down to the filter in the other.

Once, I stole a robin's egg from its nest and kept it inside a tiny jewelry box filled with cotton. When I opened the box the next morning, the egg had turned into a tiny deer. Truth is, there are no such things as ghosts.

TAJO

In his dream, Paulo marries Gloria. She doesn't see him as the thin scarecrow he is. He owns both Alpaca and Llama herds, lavishes her with the richly dyed fabric she loves to make into her dresses. He feeds her Ispi, butter beans, Lucumas. Her lips taste like heavy cream. When she looks at him, her eyes reflect the sun. Her breasts are full and warm against him. Inside her belly, their child curls in contentment.

His people are starving. Paulo wishes he could walk through the city without the fear of falling into the gaping mine pit that has swallowed the land where he was born. Hundreds of years ago, the rocks wept silver around the campfires of his people. The veins hidden under their land were rich with lead and zinc. Paulo's great-grandparents owned handfuls of herds. Now, lead poisons the children, the elders. The blue line across their gums is a tattoo marking them for death. His people call the mine *Tajo*. While they waste away, Tajo eats their houses, schools, and churches. The children's bellies wail as they walk in their sleep, searching for food in the middle of the night. They fall into the mouth of the mine. Tajo is never satisfied.

In his dream, Paulo walks toward the center of town. Houses line the street, their windows open. He can see the people inside rolling dough in preparation for a midday meal. In the yards out front, brightly colored clothes hang on sagging lines. The skirts and tunics flap like pinned birds in the breeze. He smells aging fires and hears young laughter. Paulo steps lightly past each house as he hears flutes and guitars drawing him towards town. A fiesta with a parade and *huaynitos*; village girls wearing multicolored skirts like layered flags. They beckon him to join them. He wants to dance. He is not tired or hungry.

He sees Gloria. She is twirling and stomping her feet to the music. The pink and red layers of her *polleras* bounce against her waist like crashing waves. She dances towards him, her *k'eperina*—the carrying cloth where a child would sleep—now empty. Her black hair clings to her face like a funeral shawl. Paulo reaches out to her, his hands resting on her waist as he joins the dance. People surround him as he spins Gloria around and around until he is dizzy and begins to fall into the mouth of Tajo. As he falls, the bones and skulls of his people flash past him. He squeezes his eyes shut, knowing what will come, and imagines Gloria rocking their son, her hair tickling his tiny nose as she leans over his sleeping face. She sways back and forth, up and down, her voice a siren's song as she sings of the sea: *La mar estaba serena, serena, serena.*

IF ONLY TONIGHT WE COULD SLEEP

I find you in the white swirls of the night sky, but the stars keep changing their patterns. There is no way to know if the Big Dipper was once the Little Dipper. If Cassiopeia morphed into Canis Major. When I call your name, the stars drop a little lower. They drop until they become piles on the ground. I sort through them like tangled Christmas ornaments looking for you. Every time I think I have found you, the stars disintegrate into crunchy powder in my hands. I build you a tiny house from the piles of leftover stars. It is hollow inside like a broken ribcage. I call your name while the stars continued to pile up on your house and I can hear the earth's heartbeat underneath me.

The earth stirs and whispers, *The universe will never allow you to have something so perfect.*

ONE GOOD DRESS

The river was blue before the flood. Before the rain came and didn't stop for three days. The people were blue after the river forced its way into their mouths. Your mama was still a girl. She first met your daddy at the edge of town. The weeds were eating their way past the railroad tracks. You remember your mama in her one good dress. She said, *Light my cigarette*. She said, *Light my cigarette but don't leave me.*

Your eyes were blue, like your mama's one good dress, when you left your hometown. Your brother's ghost lingered behind. You remembered when you were both still boys. How the apples on the trees turned from sweet to bitter. Your brother would pick them, cradling them like babies in his shirt. How he carried the weight for years—a burden he never wanted for you. How the heaviness became the gun he held to his head.

Blue is the color of serenity, but you know it as love's defeat. You know it as a woman lying broken on the ground, the shadow of the building she jumped from sheltering her. You say, *I wasn't worth it*. But you know better. You know because she was a jigsaw puzzle and you would put her together, someday.

You awaken in a flood of blue now. You wait for an hour, wondering how long it will take until someone notices you never showed. How long it will take before someone comes knocking on your door. The pounding of bone against wood will replace the burden of your heart.

They say your mama was buried in her one good dress. The earth was black against the blue of her hem. They say, *You can never go home again,* but you know this isn't true. Every night you lie alone in bed, the rain outside your bedroom window tapping with small fingers against the glass.

They say the river won't flood again, the waters won't swell. I say, *I love you,* and I wonder if my words are blue. The color of a fresh bruise. The color of the river before the flood. The color of the flame from the match when you lit your mama's cigarette, the embers catching on the hem of her one good dress.

MACKINAW

I see the island from where I stand now, on a ferry, drunk on waves that can easily toss me aside like a rag doll. You remember me with a tiger lily pushed behind my ear. Whatever you were thinking when you pulled it from the ground has been seized by the riptides. We planned the trip to Mackinaw months ago. I feel your absence every time the ferry rocks against the waves, jostling me. I have no one to grab on to. I imagine the water reflecting off your eyes, changing from blue to green and back to blue again. You never could make up your mind.

Passengers on the ferry are talking about the island, anticipating tasting the famous fudge and taking a carriage ride around the island, lost within *Somewhere in Time*. I see myself hiding out with the college kids that work during the summer months. I'll brush the horses down at nightfall. Tend to their stalls. Drink until early morning, long after the island has closed to tourists. Play hide-and-seek in the cemeteries where Civil War soldiers sleep. The lightning bugs, tiny, bright lanterns in the dark. Yachts dot the main shoreline, glittering like mismatched jewels, pointing their bows northeast towards an even richer land. Mansions overlook the water, wedged between rocks.

I want to stand on the ledge of a windowsill of one of the mansions, my hair slapping my face, a useless sail. I watch the ghost of myself on the windowsill ledge as I stand on the deck of this ferry, moving closer towards the island. I leave miles behind where I once tasted the sea salt off your lips, our breath jammed in our throats, my fingernails carving half-moons in your skin. The lights from the park surrounding your car hung heavy as funeral drapes. But I am a shadow now, standing on a windowsill ledge, standing on a deck of a ferry, a body readying itself. I recall my swim coach in high school reminding me to tuck my chin into my chest before I dived. Warning me that if a body strikes water hard enough, it's exactly like hitting concrete.

YELLOW

The factory lights blink a final goodnight while the workers shuffle home. The buildings are burning while the bodies sleep. There is nothing kind about home. Yellow fills the window-eyes of the factories forgotten in dusk. Stray dogs scrap over someone's discarded dinner. The walls in the lunch rooms are painted a sick yellow. The workers watch their backs. The leftover skin of nicotine and sad sandwiches. The homeless slump on their sidewalk-beds. The sound of soft chaos will lead them all home.

Early mornings and a slow sun rising won't guarantee an arrival. The men are more than yellow. Roosters crow and still birds blanket their clutch of dotted eggs. Forgotten dynamite in blistered buildings. The canaries are humming. Their ghosts are still where they left them. The dogs are watching. Listen, the eggs are cracking. They are told to stay, don't run.

They once were told yellow is the color of happiness.

THE STARS CANNOT POSSIBLY LOVE YOU

A siren in the sea wears wire for hair. When she sings an entire cosmos spills from her mouth. I point at the cosmos as it bobs on the waves. I point at your ship as you circle the planets. The siren regrets starting the universe. She says, *The stars cannot possibly love you.*

You are a sailor. You need a star to find your way home. When you touched me for the first time I turned into a star. When I touched you back with my pointy edge you became night. The only way I can exist is if you hover behind me. Sometimes I am swallowed by the sea. The light in me dies but you still find me. There is a lighthouse where I sit and direct the beam towards your ship away from the rocks. The beam of light is so bright it burns the ocean.

Stars never twinkle, you say. *It is the light from our world collapsing that makes it look like they do.*

RITUAL

My boss found out her grandbaby died. I was on the phone when I heard her scream. The lilt in her voice. As she was standing, she began to fall. The women in my area gathered around her as she cried and wailed. It felt ancient. Unspoken. We rocked together.

We told her to breathe   breathe

b r e a t h e.

I was reminded of when I was in labor with my son, breathing like she was, trying to hold her heart inside of her chest. Labor pains are a giant wave. The lull, the drag, the crash. I felt this crash inside of her, the break of it, the collapse.

FOUR MOTHERS OF DEMONS

Agrat Bat Mahlat: Mother of illusion and magic

The demons strayed and spirits hung themselves in air. The crows speak first, offering a feather here, a trinket there, a kill-skull. Rabbits curl inside womb-warm burrows. On rooftops she is on fire, dragging the dead as a net behind her. They lust. Her body is not for human or demon. They say they are one and the same. One desperate glance as she burns through night, the final countdown of hearts about to die. If you listen close, they sound just like a mother's death prayer.

Mahalath: Mother of Agrat Bat Mahlat and queen of the dancing demons

Now there are demons, wings folded like fall leaves ready to be broken. The blood from the women's thighs turns the season. Daughter streaks through the sky, mistaken for dying stars. Once, there was no one. The demons fought from their root-wombs in the trees, followed me home. Their feet bruised the earth until it scarred. A path into nothing. I do not remember when there were others here. Soon their wings will crack open, desire dripping from hoof and muzzle. They know my voice and nothing else, not even the moon killing the sun, slow and soft. It is night again and the crows cry a death song. My demons watch me, impatient like children, tongues tasting air. Waiting for me to move. For my final word to fall.

Naamah: Mother of divination, beauty, and sex

Our bodies fold together, bending, binding. Skin slides and quakes with each tiny death. The number three is the first sacred number. Shatter me with each thrust. Let our friction frenzy into a catalyst. Do you see the currents unfold before the flood? They cannot break our lust. Let the land dream of oceans, waves slipping skin over bones. They say demons die like humans. Hold your breath and count to three. Try to keep your eyes off me.

Lilith: Maiden of Desolation (in three mythologies)

Lilith Leaves Eden

Remember we were created together, one thread, broken in two. You command I lie beneath you. I killed the version of the woman you love. I have my wings. Look at you, watching me float away. A scowl and a shake, wishing we were not born as one. The Eden beneath my feet is tiny. Hell is in the faces of the lush. There is no one left to answer to. It is easy to forget. You will turn in the night and reach for me. Are you afraid? You should be. The serpent warned you with its tongue. It tastes you and whispers, *I've always loved you more.*

Lilith as Thief of Newborn Children

I perch on your windowsill, waiting for the candle to burn low. The smell of soap and fresh skin hangs in the air of your room. Do not look now, I am coming in. How do mothers do it? This comforting of flesh. Pick your head up, child, and look at my horror. *Shhh do not cry, I will tickle your feet.* Do you hear that? It is the sound of your soul smacking against the walls. Your breath playing hide-and-seek. Your skin is the perfect shade of blue. I cradle you in my wings, rub talon against cheek. I am your mother now.

Lilith as Seducer

One last dream and I have slipped inside your bed, naked and sweeping my lips across yours. My beauty makes men weep. I push you inside of me as the crows call your name, listen. You moan and gasp a terrible song. It is always the same. I want your seed, not you. I am darkness and you are nothing. Call this night a sacrament, a testament, a holy union. Call it what you will to stop the trembling. If those crows were blackbirds, you might have a chance. Blame the lost blessings, the prayers left to wander. I am your savior, your God, your coming Eucharist. Scream my name. You will remember me in the morning. When dying, they always want more.

SCARECROW

Dolly feigns death by starving herself while the others at the table take seconds from the bowl of mashed potatoes and slices of meatloaf. Mama announces there's no pie for dessert, just butter cookies. She has little tolerance left after twenty years spent as a Civil War reenactment soldier's wife. Papa never learned to clean his rifle right and blew half his scalp off, leaving Mama a widow and me an orphan. Mama spent more time crouching her way through the woods with a shotgun hunting rabbits than she did teaching me my lessons.

Dolly is my only girl and she has grown into two girls. One has eaten the other. Sunday suppers are usually spent with Great-Aunt Lila, cousin Bennie and his two boys, and occasionally Uncle Stu and Mort, his deaf and blind cocker spaniel. I spend most of my time during the meal harpooning Dolly to her seat, slapping her hands as they reach for the buttered bread rolls, the game hens, and the chocolate pudding. My husband left me four years ago for a truck stop diner waitress who wears earrings in the shape of pineapples. Mama likes to sneak Dolly caramels from her knitting bag. Dolly stares at her with adoring eyes. The kind of stare I never get. You'd think I was starving her. I tell her, *You'll thank me for this when you grow up.* That no man alive will marry her in the state she's in now: swollen and pink like a spoiled lap dog. No decent man, at least.

We never had sweets in the house. Not until Papa blew his brains out all over a Kansas cornfield. A month after his funeral, Mama told me to get in the Chevy and we bounced our way down the gravel road to the Pick 'n Save. She filled an entire grocery cart with clearance Easter candy. Breakfast was Cadbury Creme Eggs melted on top of butter-rich pancakes. Lunch was Peeps placed precariously amongst sweet potatoes, their beaks poking up like tiny mountain peaks. Supper was barely a slice of meat followed by huge lumps of ice cream topped with chocolate-covered marshmallow bunnies. After months of eating sugar, my teeth ached every time I heard a candy wrapper being opened.

I tell Dolly, *You would have such a pretty face if you just stopped stuffing your pie hole.*

When everyone hoists themselves out of their seats and retires to the sitting room, Dolly runs upstairs to the bathroom while Mama and I clear the table like we do every Sunday. Supper plates and cups are gone in a single trip. I wait until Mama is bent over the sink, her hands covered in lemon-scented suds, to sneak into the sideboard. I grab the bottle I hid earlier, tuck it inside my apron pocket, and step outside on the porch into the night. I stare at the cornfield where the scarecrow hangs, a messy Christ figure in a straw brimmed hat. The crows like to gather on him as a meeting place. Their talons grip and tear apart the faded garments that were once Papa's old button up shirt and trousers. They consider me a useless threat as I take a long swig from the flask—Maker's Mark, sometimes vodka—as they regard me. I hear Dolly crying through the open window upstairs and Mama humming as she finishes up the dishes. Uncle Stu is arguing with Great-Aunt Lila over the cost of butter beans again. I lean against the side of the porch and take another swig, eyeball the crows. They have a funny way of picking at each other's feathers. They have a funny way of cawing and squawking at each other also, like they're having a squabble. Maybe they're deciding to settle in for the night. Maybe they'll decide to fly away, taking that old scarecrow along with them.

SECRETS OF THE PLAYGROUND

We wear dresses made from city chiffon and velvet, paint our fingernails Candy Heart Pink and Lilac Swoon like our mamas. During recess we sit on the blacktop, pull strands from your scalp and braid them together. Our scabbed knees bake in the sun. We eat the hair bulbs from your roots like candy, popping them between our milk teeth, all smiles. You are new and not allowed on the swing set. You do not know the secrets of the playground. Your mama sends you to school in a red gingham dress and a homemade lunch. When the final bell rings she is waiting with a smile and a wave. Our mamas don't come for us. They sit on porches camouflaged by kudzu and observe our neighborhood with a guarded gaze. They smile with lipstick on their teeth, cradling glasses with ruby red drinks. We steal your lunch pail, toss its contents out on the lunchroom floor. You are an obnoxious puppy we love to push down. Kick dirt in your face. Tug the stitching from the hems of your dress. You don't belong with us. There *may* be a way to join us, we tell you, but it takes an act of sacrifice. We take you to the sidewalk by the monkey bars and point at the fissure in the concrete, demanding you raise your foot. Your leg is a tiny earthquake as we hold our breath, waiting for you to do what we know you can't. What we've been sing-songing to you all week. We tell you: *If you don't step on that crack, we're gonna break your mama's back.*

THREE SONGS

Upside Down

She's turning me around and round, singing *lemme me touch you down there or I won't be your friend.* I was small and fragile like the antique vases in her parent's living room, the ones we could *lookbutdon'ttouch.* We blew kisses into the emptiness and whispered little girl prayers, tugging our pigtails loose and popping pink bubblegum. We twirled and stomped bare feet, transformed into mermaids and unicorns, swearing to never return to our human selves. *Shhh*, she sang, her hands two sleepy birds cradling me, *you don't want to be a little girl forever.*

Fire Woman

Lord, have mercy, come on and shake it, so I do, his eyes on my body, a fifteen-year-old body I'm still zipping up every day like a costume, trying to make myself fit. Hands pull-push while bloated raindrops plop against the patio glass door. My cat Sheba is meowing to be let inside, a tiny black paw swatting the glass and wiping rain aside, shaking fur, wild eyes locking with mine. He has me pinned, wire-bristle beard scalding my skin. A week ago, Sheba dropped a still-struggling bird on my lap. I screamed and yelled while she skit-scat out the door but now she's back and I can't move. Her mouth open-shuts while a siren churns and wails, a stack of storm clouds layering the sky.

Jenny, I Read

Something you said about rock and roll, about life and death, words glued in my mind. So I huff but don't puff, I drag hard and pass to the left (not the right) and the smoke cloud sits heavy on my chest like my older brother when I was ten, poking at me, calling me *bratface.* Our skin twitches, we need more, and it's already been bedtime and waketime for two weeks now. I watch an orange sun fall and a red sun bounce from outside the apartment window while a man sits cross-legged on the couch and whispers, *I can see the red taillights heading for Spain.* My best friend's in the kitchen with the refrigerator door open, laughing and poking at something wrapped in plastic. Last year, a freshman at our school went missing. She's my ex's sister and isn't known to run the streets. I see her staring at me from the back bedroom, her eyes small and white. *Maddie, Maddie?* She's nodding and curling her fingers. When I follow her into the burning bedroom, I understand why the sun shifts from orange to red to orange.

MAMAS DON'T LET YOUR BABIES GROW UP IN SINGLE-PARENT HOUSEHOLDS

Define single parent.

Introduce your son to Potential Dad #1 after a safe period of six months. Watch Potential #1 as he buys your son's affection with Super Mario Bros. games and Laffy Taffy. Watch your son as he eyeballs his friends' dads as they high five after the basketball game. Stand awkwardly at Boy Scout meetings in a sea of khaki and beards. After your son googles "Dad," try to explain how you can't order a dad on the internet, even though you can order pizza and a wife. Keep your mouth shut when other parents complain about their exes and shared parenting plans.

Work three jobs and never see your son. Feel somewhat relieved that you don't have enough money to buy your son's love. Stay up at night having panic attacks about keeping him out of trouble when he turns thirteen. Read statistics on the drug abuse rate of children growing up in single-parent households. Watch YouTube videos on how to tie a tie. Consider never dating again. While meditating repeat this mantra: No man will ever love you. No man will ever love you. No man. Will ever. Love you.

Get laid before six months pass by again. Sex with strangers feels like an epidural. While you sit alone in your car with a backseat full of groceries, allow yourself three minutes to cry. Hide your smoking. Buy a dildo. Sex with a dildo feels like an epidural. Read statistics on the suicide rates of single mothers. Make a list of reasons why your son is better off with you. Smoke a bowl in the alley. Consider fucking your next-door neighbor, who seems like a great dad. Watch a YouTube video on how to talk to your kids about drugs. Pet the labradoodle at your son's friend's birthday party while the other parents discuss their last vacation to Vietnam while eating gluten-free cake from Whole Foods.

Read statistics on the suicide rates of boys raised in single-parent households. Stare at your son for hours while he's sleeping. Count each breath he takes. Make a list of reasons why he would be better off without you. Burn that list. Get up in the morning. Get up in the morning.

A GOOD WIFE

A man respects a woman as much as she respects herself.

Evelyn sets her hair, allows her slip to fall over her body. The silk is warm flesh. She takes a moment to picture his hands on her, finishes getting dressed. She has dishes from her breakfast to wash. Barry, her fiancé, expects this to be done before she leaves. He is still sleeping, his body spread-eagle and half hidden by sheets, exposing certain parts. She considers kissing him. She won't wake him. By the time she leaves Barry's house it is still early morning.

Always practice applying your lipstick in the mirror before you attempt this in public. No one wants to see a woman with sloppy makeup. A messy face is a messy wife.

Evelyn sits on the train, her purse in her lap as she carefully peels off her gloves. She applies her lipstick while the women sitting across the aisle flick their gaze at her. She knows her lipstick is perfect. When she is finished, she returns the tube to her purse and slips her gloves back on. She watches the farmland blurring by her. Cradles her curls like she is weighing fruit. Counts down the minutes in her head.

Prepare the children. They are little treasures and your husband would like to see them playing the part.

In the morning, Evelyn makes her lunch and packs it in a brown paper bag. A ham and cheese sandwich. A bruised apple. She has lived with her brother and sister-in-law since their father passed away. Most nights, when she isn't with Barry, she joins them for a quick dinner, excuses herself to her room to read or stare out the window. She can't see the city from where she lives but can recall the Empire State Building in her head. When she was nine, her father told her and her siblings everything he knew about its history. How it was built during The Depression. *Men were jumping off the same buildings they had built.* The image of the men flinging themselves off rooftops made her cry. Evelyn's mother snorted, knocking back the rest of her drink. Her hair was loose and unkempt. The ice cubes settling in her cocktail glass made sad, tiny notes as they clinked together.

Greet him with a warm smile and show sincerity in your desire to please him.

Evelyn arrives at Penn Station around nine in the morning and walks across the street to the Governor Clinton Hotel. Inside, she flashes a smile to the man behind the counter, asks him for a piece of paper and a pen. She composes a short note, making sure to loop all her L's and slash her T's. When she finishes, she folds the note into her purse, returns the pen, and walks down the block. She loves how her heels click and her footsteps bounce off the shop windows and alleyways. It reminds her she still exists. She catches herself in a shop window and pauses to fix her hair, straighten her skirt. A man in a business suit walks by, stares. When she reaches the building, she doesn't look up. She can feel its shadow melting over her. She clears her throat, adjusts her gloves. Her light brown curls bounce against her neck, soft as summer waves. She purchases her ticket to the top of the building. Presses the elevator button. Counts the numbers in her head.

A good wife always knows her place.

The wind on the observation deck is unruly as an angry child. Evelyn is wearing her Sunday best: a cream silk blouse, pleated gray skirt, church heels. A white scarf draped over her tweed coat. Mother's pearls. Barry's engagement ring is concealed under her gloves. The lavish diamond protrudes from her finger, heavy as a tombstone. Two other people are on the deck: a young man and woman, their backs turned to her, their hands woven. Pigeons circle as she steps toward the guardrail. She removes her coat, folds it over the deck wall. She pulls out the note she wrote earlier in the hotel lobby, scans the lines, pushes it neatly back inside. Sets her handbag next to her coat. She climbs over the rail and stands on top of the concrete wall. The wind picks at her, adjusting her hair and skirt, nagging bridesmaids' hands. Her scarf wiggles free from her neck, floating down to the streets below, a relinquished flag. Her legs won't stop shaking. Evelyn retreats from the wall and sits instead, her breaths coming out in fast, sharp bursts. She watches the couple embracing. They must be in love. They don't even look her way. Evelyn pushes herself up and faces the cityscape. Opens her pocketbook, takes out her makeup kit, freshens her lipstick. She clutches the pearls cradling her neck. She remembers when she was six, twirling around and around in her puffiest skirt until she collapsed, dizzy. Her older brother tugged her off the floor and towards the open bedroom window, swearing on their mother's grave that if she found the courage to jump, to just let go, she would float down just like *Alice in Wonderland*.

UNTITLED II

My lover's hands are around my neck. He says, *this is how love feels.* The ceiling is covered in roots. They are tangled and messy. They begin to flash red then green then blue like Christmas lights. I am a little girl sitting in front of the tree Christmas morning. Someone else's father is there and a mother and a brother. My hands are around the father's neck. The roots squirm down from the ceiling like soggy spaghetti. The mother asks if we want dinner now or later. I tell her I think the father is hungry. The roots turn into Christmas lights and blink Morse code. I don't know Morse code but now I understand them. They tell me to let the father go. They say, *hey, don't be so hard on him.* This is how love feels. A heaviness with no ending.

THIS NEVER GETS ANY EASIER

When the heaviness drops you don't see it coming. When you walk down the street enjoying the sun as it slides across your face. When you wrap around your lover, not knowing where your skin ends and theirs begins. When you are with your younger brother and watch while his red balloon drifts into the sky. When it is hard to breathe with the heaviness on top of you. When you feel like you are dying. When you try to wiggle your way out from underneath the heaviness but it's impossible. You discover you can reach your hands out, and as you do, you tear a chunk from the heaviness and eat it. It tastes like your favorite dessert when you were a kid. The heaviness feels light and fluffy as it finds its way inside your heart. You begin to understand.

Inside you a red balloon lets go and floats.

IMPACT

There are no planes in a western skyline. I hear you whispering stories as the cattails bob and nod as if listening. Stars take the sky hostage, hold it fast against them. My father, a silent figure, smoking his cigarette in the dark. The cherry burns bright then fades as if breathing. I can hear the river nearby. Our dog wailing caught in its current. My father found him the next morning, told me not to look. Barns are always painted red, I tell you, but you never want to hear the reason why. There's glass on the roadside and a car's side mirror. A dead deer by mile marker 54. The impact is ours and ends like it begins. Listen: my bird-mad heart is trapped in the center of you. But all you see is the blood thickening on the highway.

INCANTATION

This morning it's a bruised blue in the streets and in my head. The sound of the couple fighting in the apartment upstairs reverberates inside of my skull. The pumping of blood inside my ears never stops. I light a red candle and sprinkle black salt on the flame, ask for protection from the mind-sick wishing my heart dead. The sound of the people in the alley is a slow shuffle, a broom brushing against water-warped floors. The garbage truck honks twice before rumbling down the alley. I stand and listen, one foot in the air, hoping the snow will harden my shower-wet hair against my skull. The blood stops beating inside my ears, replaced by a slow hum. No one knows where the noise comes from. Some say aliens. Some say underground military operations. I say it's the sound of the dead sweeping down the alley as they warn me: you should listen to the crows when they talk to you.

EYE OF THE HUMMINGBIRD

My wife's blood is the color of raspberry jelly. When I shoot her in her eye it explodes in a mist from her face. I want to make peanut butter and raspberry jelly sandwiches for my lunch. My hands are covered in Kathy's blood. I wash them with soap and water. I hum a song and remember when Father and I would catch trout during the summer. Mother would cook them along with wax beans and okra. When I was eleven, Father told Mother I could shoot the eye out of a hummingbird. I finish packing my sandwiches and place them in a brown paper bag. I get in my car and set the sandwiches and my bag in the seat next to me. Mother is still sleeping when I use my key and enter her apartment. I shoot her in her eye just like Kathy. Blood sprays from her face. It is the color of the lipstick she wears when she entertains men. It's redder than it is pink. I cover her with her bed sheet and kiss her forehead. The stain from the blood is a rose that soaks into the sheet. The stain is beautiful. By the time I make it to the bank tower it is still early morning. The birds are talking in loud voices. They are trying to settle some kind of dispute. I hunker into my spot at the top of the tower wall and survey the courtyard below. People are starting their day. A mother with a baby stroller. A boy on a bike. Men in business suits. I'm not wearing my suit today. I'm wearing camouflage. Kathy ironed my outfit last night. She didn't ask why. The birds scream at the sound of the bullets as I pull the trigger. The blood splatter from the people below looks like tiny clouds. They are colors from my childhood. Strawberry lollipops. Watermelon slushies. I'm already hungry. I have four sandwiches packed. I shove the first sandwich in my mouth. It tastes like summer. I lick the jelly from my finger, put it back on the trigger. It's a beautiful fucking day alright. The sun is out. The birds are shouting. Someone is screaming from below and it sounds just like singing.

GHOSTS ARE JUST STRANGERS WHO KNOW HOW TO KNOCK

Someone sat you on their lap, held you in place. The sun pins itself in the sky, abandons you at night. If it weren't for morning you would stay on the floor. A cold spot in your bed where no one sleeps. Hunger is more than sustenance, why feed yourself? It's safer to count stars than people. A stranger outside the door you never let in. They leave you notes with one word: salvation, desire, hope. You burn them, watch as the birds freeze in flight. Believe in omens. The warm spot in your chest as something more. An empty bottle. Blow inside and make a wish. A ghost is just another lover that's forgotten your bed. The place where their head rested on heart and flesh. You know the stars are dying. Wish. When a stranger knocks, answer.

SKELETON PLOTTING

Sometime in the night the river froze. Splintered into a quilt of mirrored stars. We sleep with feet touching. Inhaling heat from fire below. The smell of our sex floats easy on pine needle winds. Curtains puff from cabin windows, touch your face with finger hems. An imaginary bear slumbers, too sleepy to growl. You blow on the ember bed, enraging its heart. Bees curl in their death pose, stiff on cold bricks. Your soft mouth finds me, is never satisfied. My legs seize, unraveling the blanket beneath us. Bullets slice the forest's armor, kills the history of trees. You smell of aging fire, my scent burning on your tongue. Remember my taste. Remember our little deaths. We are safe as roots buried beneath graves.

NOCTURNE RECALL

Toss the sun aside. Crack out the night. Let the whiskey breathe a bit first. We call this our time so bring on the flames. It's time to set the furniture on fire. Remember your father when he burned the night ticks off you with the end of his cigarette. How your skin anticipated the blister that never came. How the tick buried itself deeper in your skin. You never could stop the itch. The night always smelled of wet earth and dry grass. He is the image scorched in your head of every man you will allow to touch you. You wanted the sound of your mother's fingers on piano keys to keep tinkering. You wanted the offbeat from cold streets. The call of young mothers lit by street lights on your block. Hear their voices fly like a kite on the fourth of July. The crack of a beer can in between bottle rockets. The sound of the man screaming in the middle of the road as the tires screech. The smell of burning rubber married to asphalt that won't let go. The one road that leads into town but refuses to show you the only way out.

SACRAMENT

This is only for you. Before bridges touched one ache to another. Bodies tossed aside, forgotten dolls from tiny hands. Bridges are built to be broken. A map of empty holes. Graves for broken hearts buried chest-deep. We have known this cemetery and more. Circle the gravestone three times. Demons may hover but won't come near. Call your name and some other voice answers. We know our sacred touch, your body knotted with mine in holy bedsheets. I am not easily fooled. Those demons know this is only for you.

SMALL TALK

Outside on my smoke break there is the usual gathering of people and a few I don't know smoking and enjoying the sun. Summer clothes abound. The air smells of spray tan and Victoria's Secret perfume.

Them: *It's so nice outside. I had the best lunch ever. I love everything. And everyone.*

Me: *Did you see what happened in Civic Center Park yesterday? A guy dumped gasoline all over himself then lit himself on fire while running in handcuffs from the cops. A group of school children were walking by on their way back from a field trip and saw the entire thing.*

Them: *So, any plans for Easter?*

COPING

For Dad

It was one of those lazy Sunday afternoons when my dad decided it would be a good idea to make me watch *The Shining*. When I told him it looked scary, he said it wasn't that scary, and besides, it took place here in Colorado and it would be good for me to learn more about the history of our state. My older brother was at a friend's house blowing up bottle rockets and riding his bike, the usual weekend routine. I was happy to have him out of the apartment. My dad rented a unit out of a fourplex behind the dirt bike hills on the west side of Colorado Springs. It was known as the low-income area of town, a place where almost everyone was on government assistance and took the bus to work, leaving behind broken-down cars balanced on concrete blocks alongside battle-busted refrigerators.

My dad refused to watch cartoons and told me so as he turned the channel knob to the old black and white TV we had in our living room, displaying Jack Nicholson's car driving what I know now as the infamous Sidewinder Pass. We shared the upstairs floor with one other unit where our neighbor Carl lived. He was part of a biker gang and drove an old orange muscle car when he wasn't riding his motorcycle. Almost every weekend, Carl would get drunk and lie spread-eagle on the asphalt, laughing hysterically as his friend revved his car's engine a few yards away from him, headlights on, radio blaring Creedence Clearwater Revival. I thought it was funny. All the neighbors would yell out their windows to *keep it down, dammit!* Everyone but my dad, who stood at the front door of the duplex smoking one cigarette after another, not saying a word.

Eventually, Carl's laughter would turn into crying. I couldn't tell the difference at first until his friend revved the engine again and sped towards him, stopping within inches of his leather boots. Carl yelled at him do it, *just do it, fucking Christ!* wiping the tears from his cheeks with the back of his hands. Eventually, they both stumbled upstairs to pass out until the next weekend.

My dad never talked about Carl. I asked him once why he didn't say anything, but he just shook his head and mumbled something about how Vietnam messed with people's minds. He'd seen a lot of things when he was over there himself. Things he never wanted to talk about with me or my brother. I didn't push him to tell me. Not then and not now. But every once in a while, *The Shining* will come on TV and I'll sit down to watch old Jack holding an ax and laughing his ass off, remembering the day when Carl, spread-eagle on the asphalt, eventually stopped laughing.

UNTITLED

I'm calling you out.
You're a dream
but never a reality.
You're everywhere
on the streets and in my sheets.

I work all day and catch
the Colfax bus home at night.
You're everywhere on the bus;
your smells, your faces, your rage.

A woman
twitching in her seat
from withdrawals.
I'm too scared
to sit next to her.

I see the face
of the man who tried
to kill me every day
in my son's face.

I can't wake up.
I can't move.
The psychiatrist tells me
it's sleep paralysis but
I think it's you.

I can solve algebra equations
in my dreams

but I can't figure out
how to live
off $2300 a month
with three jobs
and a son to raise.

Soon he will lose
his Medicaid because
of a man who cares more
about the size of his hands
than the size of his heart.

No equation solves
how I can save my son
from the seizures
that are trying to kill him.

My eyes aren't brown
they're hazel
but who gives a fuck
when no one looks you
in the eye anymore?

Men tell me it's so cute
when I try to write poetry
and read in front of people.

This is how the world is, honey.

Put your big girl panties on.

You're prettier when you smile.

Swallow next time, will ya?

I can't get the smell
of bleach
out of my nostrils
that I use to scrub
the black mold
off my son's bedroom walls.

I can't scrub everything clean.

The bleach makes it look
like the mold is gone
and the walls are clean
when they're really not.

Some of us can see it
but too many of us can't.

It was never gone.

It's still here,
Growing.
Killing us
with every single breath that we take.

BURDEN

Christina cleans the building where I work. I run into her at least twice every day as she pushes her cleaning cart, white earbuds in her ears. I ask her in Spanish, *Como tu va por día ahora?* and she shakes her head, giggling. *Como va tu día por ahora?*

She and I have both been cleaning for years. We talk about how we used to clean houses, how different a mansion is from a professional building. How people would leave out piles of change and bills someplace obvious, just to see. Swapping our best worst stories. Exploding toilets. The time I had to scoop shit out of a urinal. I lost the coin flip that day.

I watched one of the managers talking to Christina the other day in the hallway by the cafeteria. The woman was wearing a navy pantsuit and beige shoes with square heels. She held a yellow sticky note in her hand and pointed at the tiles lining the hallway floor by the bathrooms.

I need this floor to be dry before eight am, does that make sense?

Yes.

Because people can slip and fall if the floors are still wet. Does that make sense?

Yes.

The toilet paper also needs to be replaced every hour, not every two hours.

Sí.

Excuse me?

Sí. Yes.

When the weather is cold, Christina rubs her elbows. She says, *Ouch! It hurts to scrub today.*

There has never been a day that has gone by when I didn't see her pushing her cleaning cart, sweeping the front steps, picking up the cigarette butts people toss because they're too fucking lazy to use the ashtrays.

I don't trust anyone who's never had to clean up someone else's shit, she says, pulling a yellow glove over each of her hands.

SHOWTIME

On Christmas morning everyone in America opens the same gift. The gift is inside a box with a red ribbon tied around it. You open the box and look inside. It is a diorama of the cemetery scene from *Beetlejuice*. You pull it out and set it down on the floor in front of you. There are several graves with tombstones surrounded by a cemetery fence. Instead of Michael Keaton, the bully from when you were a kid is standing on the hilltop wearing the same black-and-white striped suit as Beetlejuice. A sign is next to them but instead of flashing BETELGEUSE it says AMERICA.

Your bully points at the sign and then the graves. You look closer and realize each tombstone has the name of every dictator that has ever lived.

It's showtime, your bully says.

ME AND MY BOY

Go on and say something
while I sit here.
I can wait all damn day

and I have waited patiently
by my boy's hospital bed,
his head wrapped in gauze
while neurons synchronize
their fire in his brain.

I have laid hands upon him
not in a moment of evoking God
not in a moment of playing Paul
with his brother Saul

When lightning strikes
if you touch the ground
you can feel it vibrate in your bones
There is strength in those throes

for a body to survive
one hundred seizures in a night

For a body to survive at all.

And hey, kid. I know your name is Billy. Billy strikes me
as a pussy kind of name. And if you're old enough to push
him down, if you're old enough to kick and punch him, then
maybe I should call you Bill. Notice my son never says a
word. Even when you tell him he should just kill himself.
There's strength in coming back from the dead. It follows

my son, lingering behind his footsteps. I see it every day in his face. Maybe there are a million excuses why you are who you are. Give me a reason why I shouldn't grab you by the back of your hair and push you out of this bus. Watch as you tumble and fall.

But my boy has his hand on my hand. And even though he's twelve he's not embarrassed to hold the hand of his mother. I feel the tempo of his pulse beating into mine.

We sit.

Me and boy, we don't say a word.

DONOR

For Tim

In the hospital lobby is a giant cardboard cutout of a cartoon bear with the words PLEASE BEAR WITH US WHILE WE'RE UNDER CONSTRUCTION! It's my second trip to the hospital in less than a week and I figure it's only a matter of time before no one is watching or waiting in the lobby, allowing me the opportunity to kick the shit out of the cardboard bear. I'm carrying two large pizzas and three smaller boxes of cheesy bread. In my backpack is a four-pack of Coke. I can't remember which elevator to take so I ask a nurse. She gives me directions to the ICU, and I wander the hallways while visitors and staff all smile at the pizza boxes and make comments like, *Oh is that for me?* and *You're so nice to bring me food!* I keep walking until I find the waiting room. Hand sanitizer stations are mounted to each wall in sets of five with small panels displaying snot-green gel. The room smells like the Wendy's bathroom on Colfax; bleach and anxiety. A man is sitting at a table surrounded by fifty empty tables. My family is nowhere to be found. He glances up, agitation crossing his face. Behind him a window displays a storm cloud sliding across an empty blue sky. I'm not the doctor with the news he's been waiting all day to hear. I force a smile, just for him. It isn't anywhere near as small and polite as I intend it to be. I set the pizza down on the closest table. Somewhere in the seating area across the hall, a phone goes off blaring Cyndi Lauper's "Time After Time." The same song was playing on the radio the night I drove into a herd of more than fifty deer on the San Juan Skyway on my way back to Durango. The smell of wet leaves and hot rubber hung in the air. My headlights reflected the terror in the herd's eyes as I swerved to the right then the left, maneuvering my way past several massive bucks, slender does, and speckled fawns. I can't remember how I wound up sitting on the side of the highway, untying my shoelaces, smoking a cigarette and searching my pockets for a cell phone I didn't own. It's funny what your brain chooses to keep and what it decides to throw away.

My stepmom, dad, and sister-in-law, Kristen, walk into the room all at once. We hug, exchange *howareyous*, and sit down at the table. Huge smiles. Their faces are worn, the kind of quick-weathered look a face undergoes when overloaded with trauma. We don't talk much; busy cramming our mouths full of pizza and cheesey bread and chugging down Cokes. In another moment, we could have been sitting at a wooden picnic table in a park, swatting summer flies, watching dogs squirm in wet grass, and kids piss their red cotton shorts. Clouds puff and roll across a cotton-candy-colored sky and someone's kite catches on fire. I'm anxious to see my stepbrother, so Kristen leads me through a series of twisting hallways until we reach his room. He's lying in bed, chest bare and a Y-shape carved into his torso held together by staples the size of my thumbnail. He reminds me of the guy from the Operation game, pinned with all of his organs on display. There's a dead man's liver sewn inside of him, fighting to stay. He tells me he wants to thank the donor's family. There's a look in his eyes that's familiar but I can't place. *There will be time*, Kristen assures him. A cotton washcloth covers his forehead and I notice his skin is no longer yellow. I attempt a few jokes, stacks of sobs waiting to crash in on me, but it's a poor attempt. His eyelids are drooping, signaling my time to go. As I leave the room, I hear the beeps of machines and forced air and shoes squishing down linoleum. An intercom somewhere in the hallway demands code blue; code team, code blue, code team, and I remember where I saw that look in my stepbrother's eyes. It's funny what your brain chooses to keep and what it decides to throw away.

SERVICE

A guy who works in my office sexually harassed me. He wasn't fired after HR investigated. It was my word against his. He started bringing a service dog to work every day. Because you know, he suffers from anxiety and shit. That's what's up.

BIGGER

The peaches and apples in the grocery store are huge. I place a quarter against an apple to give a reference of size, but it became lost in the galaxy that is Huge Fruit. I ask a few other shoppers if they're alarmed at how big the fruit is today, but they just stare at me. I watch the clerk's face carefully in the checkout line, waiting for his reaction when he scans the gigantic fruit. Nothing. I ask him why the fruit is so fucking huge. Why? *That's how things are now. People's mouths are getting bigger too. And words. Words are goddamn enormous.* He then tells me he doesn't get paid enough to explain giant fucking fruit. *Maybe don't eat it,* he says.

THE WIVES

The wives don't give a shit about your degrees or the fake Klimt and Van Gogh on your walls. They live in Victorian homes because they married the men who were sexy nerdish back in the '90s, make one hundred thousand a year now, and somehow seem much more attractive. The wives size you up like they regard themselves in full-length mirrors in the dressing rooms of Macy's or Nordstrom.

You don't fit.

You use their bathroom and open the medicine chest and the cupboard under the sink, notice the expensive tampons and the boutique makeup in pretty cases. You eat the sliced cheese spread out on the cutting block and decline the prosciutto, raising eyebrows.

The wives' husbands share a look, the same look you got from your daddy's friends when you were twelve.

Your girlfriends back in your hometown all empathize with you. But you don't tell them that when the wives are away on vacations, their husbands come to visit you. They bring you their wives' dresses to try on before they fuck you on the mattress you salvaged from the alley behind your apartment.

They tear the fabric off your body, not caring how much it costs. They tell you it fits you just like a glove.

PLAYDATE

My son has a playdate today with a boy named Abraham. This means Abraham's parents, Michael and Barb, will be interviewing me. Parents always need to determine if their kid will be kidnapped, dismembered, or have words like *douchebag* added to their child's vocabulary as a result of hanging out with someone else's kid.

Abraham's mom and dad are still married. They throw the occasional wine party with their neighbors in their foyer, which is decorated with busted historic farm tools. The neighbors' children, like Abraham, are named after dead presidents or obscure musical notes. I chose to name my son after a dead rock star. Despite our social and economic differences, I am willing to bet that my college degree will allow them to bypass their initial fears. Michael and Barb will take notice of my alma mater and tell their neighbors over a primordial bottle of pinot noir: *She is a Single Mom, but she is educated.* Bet your ass, Mike and Barb. I am credible, smart enough to know about GMOs while label-hunting boxed mac and cheese for artificial ingredients like riboflavin that will liquefy Abraham's gastrointestinal tract. While Barb nibbles on the sliced cheese sweating on my coffee table, Michael and I will discuss the diverse hardships of undergrad and grad schools, segue into how we both wound up at the Lollapalooza concert (the one without Jane's Addiction) by some shoestring twist of fate, and laugh, caught up in our own reveries, realizing how adulthood has killed our teen spirits.

I want Michael and Barb to walk into my house and overlook the mismatched thrift store furniture. My throw blankets, draped like buttercream over the love seat, hide the imperfections in the wood and tired fabric. I question whether to take down my Klimt painting before their arrival. She is a naked woman—ethereal and mesmerizing—but she is flashing her blimp-sized breast which takes up a quarter of the painting. When is a breast artistic enough to still be considered a breast and not a *boob? Fun bag?* She may be too porno.

The next step will involve ushering Michael and Barb through my hallway, living room, and kitchen, assuming my role as tour guide. *See all my books? See how clean my house is? No crack pipes or needles here, folks.* This house is a careful collaboration of yard sale scavenger hunts and thrift store discounts—discarded items no longer wanted. I give them a home again, place them in tiny rooms like doll furniture, playing out scenes and rearranging them. Should Michael and Barb ask where I work, I will politely respond that I *wear many hats.* Truth be told, I am not sure I want to tell them about the posh houses I clean as a maid. How I scrape other people's crusted piss off toilet rims. That while changing bed sheets, to my horror, the amount of pubic hair that a person sheds can be found in even the highest thread counts, like tiny stubborn fish hooks. There are ghosts that live within the walls I clean. I see the resident monsters hidden under the beds, in closets, behind couches. I scrub them, dust away the layers of age, or pretend they don't exist.

Barb may touch my elbow like she's picking up a broken glass and ask about my son's dad. To break the tension she'll smile, show me the best parts of her teeth—the insurance paid parts—her tongue delicately tapping the expensive inlays. I will assure her that although my son has no Positive Male Role Model in his life because his dad is, in fact, a Piece of Shit, he still has several male figures to look up to. I have many friends he likes to call uncle. She will bob her head and cross-stitch her eyebrows like she totally gets it, but she doesn't get it. Why tell her about the handfuls of men who sometimes cooked me breakfast in the morning, played video games with my son, showed *interest*—only to be thrown out at 2:00 a.m. Guys like Steve, who pawned my son's Nintendo DS for drugs. Mike left his phone sitting next to me while random texts from Cindi and Sarah popped up with questions about sex and money. Then there was Nathan, who punched a hole in my wall in a fit of rage, emphasizing his words: *stupid* and *bitch*. Instead, I will smile and nod, knowing in the wisdom I have acquired only through a support group kind of pain that there really is no way of explaining to this woman that I am a mom, just like her.

My son has a playdate today, so I push back his curtains and raise his window to let more of the light in. He confronts me, anxious for Abraham to arrive and demanding to know where I hid his dinosaur model of a Spinosaurus—much more of a prehistoric badass than a T-Rex ever was. He hopes to have an epic dinosaur battle. He takes my hand as we explore his room, telling me about all the fun games they can play, the baking soda volcano they can make in order to unleash the final demise of the dinosaurs. I nod my head as I look around his room. I notice the walls show cracks and are shedding their painted skin. I recall how the landlord assured me that although this old Victorian has a lot of history, it also has character. The bones are unbreakable. I flatten my palm against the bumpy painted interior, knowing if it happened to be haunted, if the ghosts were still attached to the flaking walls, I can live with them.

THEY TASTED LIKE THE DOLLAR STORE CANDY I BOUGHT MY SON EVERY YEAR AT XMAS

When he called to cancel our date, I told him I understood. The fake smile stretched my lips out and I had to rub chapstick on them afterwards. That night, after checking the cupboards one last time, I bit each nail off and spit them on the floor. The purple tasted bitter and the gemstones were slightly salty. It may have been the glue.

CAKE BY THE OCEAN

He tells you to bring him cake, the one with the sweet frosting. You go home, put together ingredients in a bowl, and use the last of your sugar for the frosting. You bring it to him, watch as he cuts a piece with a knife. You know it's perfect. The frosting is bone white. He eats one bite then sets the plate aside, retreats to the bedroom. You trail after him, enter the bedroom just as he turns the light off. When you slide yourself next to him, the warmth of his skin burns. You know he's naked. You're still wearing the dress you had on last night when you baked the cake. You smell of vanilla and warm milk. The bedroom is silent except for a fly buzzing in the window and the sound of the spray of ocean waves rolling in, rolling out. There are parts of the sea that are too deep to descend. Creatures that have never seen light and where water surpasses black. Color has no meaning in places where light doesn't exist. His bedroom is that place now. You feel the space between your skin and his vibrate. The area between his hand and your body could be the length of a breath exhaled. Short enough to reach over and drag your dress off. Everything behaves different in the dark. It's hard to tell where your feet will fall, where the water will carry you. It's the distance between the bottom of the ocean and where the sun resigns to hang itself.

BABY, BABY

I want to fall in love
with someone who promises
to catch me
before the wind pushes me
right over the edge.

Swears it's the sugar in my tea
that makes it taste funny.

Tells me *baby, baby, shhh*
they know this road and its curves
like the back of their hand
while my curves rest
in their hands
as they let go of the wheel and promise
to swallow me whole.

Keeps a light on for me
in their apartment in Cap Hill
where the trans woman named Queen
hung herself
from broken nylon stockings
with a torn heart.

Where we spend our nights
knotting the bedsheets
while the meth head upstairs
vacuums the carpet away
before blowing her brains clean.

It's easy to stand
on the concrete ledge
of the balcony,
the perfect size
for stiletto heels
still wobbling
from whiskey and Cokes
the night before.

Promise me
there's no wind,
the weather is perfect
for a stroll
around the ledge
of a balcony
in early morning.

Hands soft as pavement
as they push,
a voice thick as air
between my legs
whispering
baby, baby, shhh.

ACETONE

I spent the week's grocery money on getting my nails done for a first date. Peruvian Purple with tiny fake gemstones placed on top of each nail. Later, out back of my apartment, I stuck my hands in the sunshine as I smoked a cigarette. I watched as the confetti of gemstones caught the sun's rays. I was pleased at how expensive I must look.

ROAD KILL

Eighty-one miles to Cheyenne. My Lyft passenger, Judy, wanted me to take her as far as I could to the border. We pass a Motel 6 and I'm reminded of the transgender woman named Candy I worked with at the Super 8 off the highway in the Springs. She told me that one out of every four rooms we clean would have a sex toy twisted in the sheets. She was right. She'd moved from Chattanooga to Colorado, said the miles weren't enough. Said the two-bedroom apartment she shared with three other transgender folks was enough. Fifty-seven miles to Cheyenne. Judy said she was leaving her husband after twenty years. *Cheatin' bastard*, she called him. I was reminded of the Patsy Cline song. You know which one. She checked her makeup in a lighted compact mirror every few minutes. She did nothing to fix the melting mascara stains under her eyes. *I'd rather be the person cheating with than the person being cheated on*, she said. *That sounds like a Patsy Cline song*, I told her. *Yeah, only difference is she saw her wall coming at her before she hit it.* Thirty-two miles to Cheyenne and I pulled over at the truck stop diner Judy had pointed to. Her fingernails were filed into points and painted Peony Pink. She smelled like a Walmart makeup aisle. *Sorry, I can't go any further*, I told her. *Me either*, she said, tugging at her tan pantyhose under her skirt. Forty-four miles to Denver and I remembered the first sex toy I found in the Super 8. *Folks like to come here for their temporary thrills*, Candy told me. *No one's going to love you in the morning here, Sugar Pie.* I turned off my Lyft app and lit a cigarette, changed the music to old Tom Waits songs. I thought about the night I quit the Sup 8. A man old enough to be that girl's granddaddy slipped into room three with a black suitcase and a six-pack of Banquet. Candy and I had to clean the room the next day. *Your cheatin' heart,* Candy sang, pointing a sad, sagging dildo at me as she stripped the bedsheets. *Will make you weep.*

HIDE-AND-SEEK

I rest my head against the window of the Colfax bus and rock as we hit potholes. My son leans against me, his face beaded with sweat from a hot day at school. The sound of the woman's voice next to me describes to her boyfriend what it was like when she was growing up. Pot of beans simmering on the stove, homemade tortillas, the smell of food filling her house. She watched her brothers and sisters while her parents worked. Helped them with homework, swept the floors, and folded the laundry by the time they returned home. When she was bone tired, she had the comfort of her family. I see expensive new vehicles fresh from the car wash, glimmering like freshly minted coins. The mansions lining 6th Ave with high-end brick and mortar. Marble pillars, bay windows, stone turrets topping patterned rooftops. I ask my son, *What do you think they do with all that room?* My son shrugs, says, *They're always playing hide-and-seek from each other.*

CLEAN

I'll never understand why people act so weird around the cleaning people. Like Christina, the woman who cleans the office building I work in. She and I talk about all kinds of shit. She tells me about her kids and what she's planning on doing for the weekend. How her bones hurt when it's cold outside and it makes it hard to scrub sometimes. I tell her how I was hit in the leg with a shot put in junior high and every time it's going to rain, I feel an ache in that one spot, the spot that would have caved in if the ball of steel hurtling at my leg hadn't bounced first. *Some aches are good, some bad,* she says.

I used to clean rich people's houses. I didn't make any more money than I did cleaning out trailer homes, but the pay was more consistent. Someone told me that Leonardo DiCaprio owned a house near the neighborhood I was working in, but I didn't give a shit. They were all the same to me. I cleaned for a woman who owned a mansion in the foothills who used to travel all over the world collecting various souvenirs as if she had a giant net the size of the ocean, catching and dragging everything behind her. A British phone booth stuffed with expensive shoes. An entire bathroom counter cluttered with antique perfume bottles, soap, and makeup. I had to dust each bottle individually or she would call me out on it. She wiped down all her bathrooms and the kitchen, left vacuum lines in the carpet before I showed up. I could still smell the bleach under a blanket of Caribbean Waters room deodorizer spray. She would pose herself in front of the mirror in the living room, fanning her nails out in front of her, adjusting her outfit. *I have a cocktail party tonight,* she would say, blowing on her nails.

The woman standing awkwardly between Christina and me in the women's bathroom washes her hands with one pump of soap as we laugh about the differences between office building, move-out, and house cleanings. She makes sure we hear her when she says, *I always pick up the paper towels that fall on the floor, just so you know.*

There were family homes I cleaned in addition to mansions. Regular people with families who worked nine-to-five jobs. One of my regular people clients was a newly married couple, Scott and Beth, and Beth's daughter. I remember changing the sheets on the couple's bed, pulling back the comforter and seeing a puddle of semen still soaking the sheets. After my short time working at a pay-by-the-hour motel off the highway, nothing shocked me. Four months after I began cleaning their house, Beth called to tell me she would be discontinuing my service. It was right after I had managed to get the routine down to two hours, knowing the shower stall in the master bedroom always took at least thirty minutes to remove all of the soap scum and the basement had to be vacuumed twice before the cat hair would come up. Scott had died two weeks prior from brain cancer. It took him fast. I remembered the semen on the sheets, a billion cells spent and dead like he was now. I felt a sick feeling in my stomach. I recalled a similar twinge of nausea hitting me after cleaning a room littered with sex toys left over from a one-nighter at the Sup 8. Two people, no matter who they are, can share a bed together and still wind up alone.

I'll never understand why people act so weird around the cleaning people. If anything, we should be acting weird around you.

COSPLAY

You are a guest on *Dr. Phil.* The theme of the show is "People Who Live Inside Dead Animals and the Partners Who Love Them." You look down at yourself and see you are inside the carcass of a deer. Your hands and feet are its hooves. Your skin is warm hide. Your head has two giant antlers pointing in all directions. One of the antlers is pointing directly at Dr. Phil's eye as he leans over to study you. You notice that he has not trimmed his nose hair in a very long time. He is telling the audience something is wrong with you and the other guests. He says this while sweeping one of his small hands in your general direction. You look to your right and see your partner smiling at you. Your partner is a beautiful white swan. Their wing reaches out and sweeps over your hoof in a gesture of pure love. You look to your left and see other couples: a red fox and a hound dog, a dolphin and a flamingo, a horse and a brown bear. The audience is scowling. They are shaking their heads in disbelief. Dr. Phil is talking in a loud voice but gradually becomes quieter. The audience leans in to hear him. You look at Dr. Phil and notice his nose hairs have started to take over his face. His small hands are becoming even smaller. After a few minutes of staring at Dr. Phil, you see he has been hiding inside the carcass of a hedgehog all along. He leans towards you and in a tiny voice says, *I've always felt safe in small spaces.*

THE SMALLEST STAR IN THE UNIVERSE IS MEANT ONLY FOR YOU

For Jay

A heart is a sponge soaked with Tropical Punch Kool-Aid. Sometimes the sponge beats and stains your countertops and floors. Your favorite Minor Threat T-shirt. Our brains are starved of oxygen so take the few moments between seizures to recognize how different the kitchen lights look from the vantage point of the floor. People bless you with hand and eye, neurons and misfires. That's all love is, a lost signal searching for its starting point. Imagine a heart that beats just for you, driven by sugar and early Saturday morning cartoons. Remember hearing a story once, long ago, about a prince and a princess, but you never made it to the ending. The bomb outside was too busy shaping the perfect mushroom cloud and the mannequins next door never knew what hit them. The first person you kissed died twenty years later in an empty bathtub searching for a needle. *Honey, I love you,* they wrote. You feel the itch but can't scratch it. This is why you live. Somewhere, a mother that is not your own is singing a lullaby. She sings a lullaby, a death prayer. The only prayer God answers. The one that apologizes for all her absences in return for one small favor.

Who's there?

ACKNOWLEDGMENTS

"A Small Infestation Following a Big Stroke of Luck" (2014), "Lullaby" (2017) Published in *Monkeybicycle*.

"Things They Don't Talk About in Parenting Class" (2014) Published in *Dogzplot*.

"Runt" (2014) Published in *NANO Fiction*.

"Play Date" (2014) Published in *Citron Review*.

"Examination" (2016) Published in *Bartleby Snopes*.

"Bottle Rockets" (2016) Published in *WhiskeyPaper*.

"I Lost My Orgasm" (2015), "Three Songs" (2018) Published in *Hobart*.

"Bang, Snap!" (2016) Published in *Cease, Cows*.

"Praise the Lord and Pass the Ammunition" (2016) Published in *Five Pure Slush*.

"One Good Dress" (2019) Published in *Pulpmouth*.

"A Good Wife" (2016) Published in *The Airgonaut*.

"Tajo and His Bones" (2016) Published in *Gone Lawn*.

"Saba on the Shore" (2016) Published in *decomP magazinE*.

"Scarecrow" (2016) Published in *Fried Chicken and Coffee*.

"Secrets of the Playground" (2016) Published in *Spelk*.

"Wild Hares" (2016) Published in *Cleaver Magazine*.

"Eye of the Hummingbird," (2016) "Service" (2016): Published in *(b)oink*.

"Huckleberry" (2017) Published in *Flash: The International Short-Short Story Magazine*.

"Somewhere There is a Field Where the Birds Will Die for You" (2017) Published in *Resurrection of a Sun Flower*.

"Mackinaw" (2016) Published in *Ratt's Ass Review*.

"Paladin" (2016), "Coping" (2018) Published in *Cowboy Jamboree*.

"Loss Aversion" (2016), "Ghosts Are Just Strangers Who Know How to Knock" (2017) Published in *Hobo Camp Review*.

"Supertramp" (2016), "Ghosts" (2016), "I answer the missed connections on Craigslist because I don't want people to feel alone and I don't want to feel alone either" (2016) Published in *Mutiny Info Reader*.

"Untitled" (2017) Published *Live Nude Poems*.

"Final Trumpet" (2018) Published in *Heavy Feather Review*.

"If Only Tonight We Could Sleep" (2017), "Rockabye Sweet Baby James" (2017), "This Never Gets Any Easier" (2017), "People Call You a Space Cowboy" (2017) Published in *Sargasso Magazine*.

"Sacrament and Incantation" (2017) Published in *Moonchild Magazine*.

"Four Mothers of Demons" (2018) Published in *Occulum*.
"Donor" (2018) Published in *Jellyfish Review*.
"Northern Lights" (2019) Published in *Lost Balloon*.
"You Can Always Come Back" (2019) Published in *Entropy*.
"Yellow and Bigger" (2019) Published in *Hairstreak Butterfly Review*.
"Holes" (2019) Published in *South Broadway Ghost Society*.

Thank you to Sean H. Doyle and Michael J. Seidlinger. Without you both, this book never would have happened. Janice Lee and the editors at The Accomplices and Civil Coping Mechanisms for making this an easier process than I imagined. To my family. To my writing family: Steven Dunn, whose valuable insight and help with this collection gave me the motivation to push forward. Kathy Fish for being a mentor and friend over the course of these stories. Your wisdom and encouragement mean the world. Thuyanh Astbury, Brian Lupo, Emma Arlington, Ahja Fox, Tameca L. Coleman, Eric Baus, Kathy Fish, Khadijah Queen, Chip Livingston, Jenny Shank, Rachel Weaver, Deanna Rasch, Erika T. Wurth, Shoshana Surek, Corey Ryan, April Bradley, Gay Degani, Robert Vaughn, Paul Beckman, Audra Kerr Brown, Anne Weisgerber, Jan Elman Stout, Nan Wigington, Linda Niehoff, Jolene McIlwain, David Hicks, Andrea Rexilius, and Marty McGovern. Your tremendous support and help with my writing will never have a big enough thank you. Stephanie Maney, who knows my heart. Charly Fasano and Nancy Stohlman for supporting me from the beginning. To my son, who teaches me to be strong and courageous. And to my partner in crime, Jay Halsey, for all the love, support, and the encouragement you've given to me over the years.

ABOUT THE AUTHOR

Hillary Leftwich is the poetry and prose editor for *Heavy Feather Review* and runs At the Inkwell Denver, a monthly reading series. Currently, she freelances as a writer, editor, writing workshop instructor, and guest instructor for Kathy Fish's Fast Flash Workshop. She lives in Colorado with her partner, her son, and their cat, Larry.